Santa Monica Baby

Kelly Reynolds

Contents

Author's Note

Santa Monica Baby is the third (and sadly, final) book in Holidays in L.A. series, though it can be read as a standalone. This low angst, high heat romance novella between a fiery, Elle Woods inspired woman and her plus-size, cinna-daddy-dom takes place between Thanksgiving and Valentine's Day.

Please be advised that this book is an **open-door** romance, meaning there is **on-page, explicit** sexual content (between consenting adults), including oral sex, vaginal sex, anal play, spanking (in a variety of ways), roleplaying, and light bondage. Mature readers only.

I've been dying to write a big boy for years. I've been obsessed with *Santarotica* just as long.

Austin is the best of both worlds.

Enjoy.

*To all the **girls** who watched "The Holiday" and fell in love with Jack Black.*

*And all the **women** who watched "Violent Night" and dreamed of sucking David Harbour's candy cane.*

Chapter One

November 28th

Nellie

"What kind of sociopath signs up to run three miles on Thanksgiving morning?"

My older sister's teasing words instantly warmed my heart, a much-needed antidote for the forty-something-degree temperatures. Leighton had never been one to mince her words. On the contrary, she had the kind of bold bluntness that made grown men quiver with fear . . . or attraction, in the case of her British behemoth of a boyfriend, Killian. It had been nearly a year since she'd moved in with the former soccer star, and he still looked at her like she was the strawberry jam to his scone.

Fuck, I could really go for a scone right now.

I probably should have eaten something before my Lyft ride over to 3rd Street, but it was too late now. Besides, three miles was a drop in the bucket for a seasoned runner like me, and there would be plenty to eat later. That didn't make me want a scone any less *now*, though. Just the thought of Bowie's turkey pot pie made my stomach growl.

"Aw, thanks, princess," Killian cooed against my sister's neck. "That's sweet."

"A donut would be sweeter," she grumbled.

A smile crept across my face as I bent forward to adjust my compression socks—brown with orange stripes to match the cartoon turkey on my race bib. Apparently, I wasn't the only one who had shown up hungry to the Santa Monica Turkey Trot.

Killian wrapped his arms around Leighton's middle, and she instantly relaxed back against his athletic frame. "How about we stop off at Donut King on the way home and grab you a couple of maple bars?"

"What if they're closed?"

He tilted her chin up with two fingers. "Then I'll figure out how to make you some at home."

She leaned up on her toes. "Mm, now you're talking, killjoy," she whispered against his lips.

Ugh, I've never felt so single in my life.

That wasn't necessarily a bad thing. Contrary to public opinion, I thoroughly enjoyed being single. There was nothing quite like coming home to *my* bed and *my* snacks in *my* apartment after a ten-hour day of contracts and spreadsheets. Besides, my morning jogs and long work hours—made longer as of late because, unbeknownst to many, the winter holidays marked the busiest time of year for lawyers—didn't leave much room for recreational activities. Thankfully, my bedside drawer full of battery-operated devices filled that . . . hole.

I still dated here and there, but love was not part of my five-year plan. Dick appointments, maybe, but those were easy to come by in a big city like Los Angeles. As one might imagine, the dating pool in Plain, Ohio—a real place, believe it or not—was slim to none, limited to the same fifty people you graduated high school with—half of whom had already married each other by twenty-two—and their divorced dads.

That would have made for an awkward morning while living with my parents.

No, love would have to wait. Relationships took time and energy, both of which I wasn't willing to spare, especially if they came at the expense of achieving my goals by the time I was thirty.

That didn't make me any less thrilled that my sister had found her forever person, though. Killian was a Ken doll come to life—British edition—and together, they were sweeter than my mom's banana pudding. It was hard to believe that just last Christmas, the two of them had faked an engagement to win over our parents, and now here they were, sucking face and living together in a mansion by the beach.

The Hollywood dream.

They made quite the power couple: all-star soccer player turned coach and budding knitwear designer. Just last month, one of Leighton's designs—a crocheted romper from her *Crochella* line—had gone viral on social media after a tween popstar had worn it on stage during a concert. Leighton had woken up the next morning to nearly two hundred online orders, a collaboration offer from a very well-known content creator, and an invitation to participate in *Snow Place like L.A.*, a winter fashion showcase.

"I'm going to go scope out a spot near mile two as soon as Nora gets back," Leighton said when she came up for air.

"Where did she disappear to?" Killian asked.

I pointed toward the parking lot, set back beyond the hundred or so racers lining up for our run. "I think she went to grab an extra jacket from the car."

Nora had thin blood, a result of being born and raised in Los Angeles. As far as I was concerned, a brisk fifty-eight degrees was the perfect temperature for a morning jog. To Nora, it might as well have been a polar vortex.

"Speaking of jackets, I need to reschedule our shopping trip to the Galleria."

The smile fell from Leighton's face. "Again?"

I shrugged. "Sorry, Leigh. One of the senior partners—"

"The rude one or the one who smells like soup?"

"Tabitha isn't rude. She's . . . impatient."

I didn't bother addressing the rest of her question. Scott, the other senior partner and Tabitha's brother-in-law, did in fact smell like soup. Campbell's tomato, to be exact.

"Anyway, she's scheduled my one-on-one performance review between the two of us that afternoon, and it *has* to go well." I clenched my fists, enjoying the sharp sting of my freshly painted nails digging into my palms. "I will not let nepotism win."

Leighton hadn't been the only Wheatley making life-changing moves this past year. I had accepted an offer from an entertainment law firm in Beverly Hills back in January, and after ten months of late nights spent staring at spreadsheets until my vision blurred, needy senior partners and even needier clients—fraudsters and murderers had nothing on struggling actors, or even worse, screenwriters—I was *this* close to nabbing the Bennett Studios account.

As in Brooks Bennett. *The* Brooks Bennett.

The former teen heartthrob had launched a boutique production company a few years back and was now looking to lock down new representation before the end of the year. My firm's partners, Wilson, Treger, and Faison—better known around West Los Angeles as *WTF*—had been "courting" Bennett Studios like the long lost

Bridgerton brothers since mid-August, and *when* we landed them as a client, the account would go to me or Scott's son.

Fucking nepotism at its finest.

Geoffrey "formerly Jeffrey" Wilson. The arrogant douche nozzle had changed the spelling to make himself seem "more cosmopolitan," his words, not mine. The only thing cosmopolitan about Geoffrey—or *Ge-offer-y*, as I called him behind his back—was the pink drink he enjoyed during our biweekly company happy hours.

The Bennett account was as good as mine. Even now, I could practically taste it, and it tasted like salty ocean spray and sweet revenge. The retainer fee alone would be enough to pay my monthly rent, and my bungalow apartment in Santa Monica wasn't cheap. It was rent-controlled, though, which was about as rare as snow in Los Angeles, so there was no way I would be moving out anytime soon.

Regardless, there was nowhere else I would rather be. The cozy one-bedroom unit was everything I had ever envisioned for myself, from the yellow buttercream paint throughout to the clawfoot tub and Tiffany-blue-tiled bathroom that looked like something straight out of a Doris Day movie.

Heeled boots clacking against the pavement drew my attention.

"Great news," Nora called out to us, navigating her way through a sea of racers and nearly knocking a pilgrim in Nikes to the pavement. "Seriously, you're going to love me."

Between her fluffy blue bomber jacket and matching blue shag, she looked like the Cookie Monster personified.

Annnd now I want a cookie. Dang it.

My sugar addiction knew no bounds.

"We already love you," Leighton told her.

"Well then, prepare worship at the altar of me." As if conjured from the heavens above, Nora produced a drink tray full of to-go coffee cups. "I found coffee."

Leighton lifted her arms toward the dark sky. We were still a good thirty or so minutes away from sunrise. "Hear ye, hear ye," she called out to the heavens. "Bless this woman and her beans."

She snatched a cup from the cardboard tray. Nora handed the other two to Killian and me before taking the last for herself.

I frowned at the name scrolled on the side of my cup. "Um, who is Hannah and why do I have her coffee?"

Killian's brows furrowed. "And how did you find coffee on your way to the parking lot?"

"I didn't," Nora answered, smiling wickedly. "I stopped the first person I saw carrying coffee and offered her fifty bucks."

"And that worked?" Killian asked.

"Not at first. But then she recognized me." Nora had gotten her big break as one of the stars of *Andromeda 8*, Hulu's Emmy-nominated space opera. It wasn't unusual for people to recognize her. "You know, people ask me for photos and autographs all the time, but this was my first ever custom voice message request."

"And what kind of message did Hannah want you to send?" I asked before sipping from the cup clasped between my palms, smiling to myself when the swirl of sugar and cinnamon met my tongue.

Hannah has exquisite taste in holiday beverages.

"Let's just say that her soon-to-be ex-boyfriend isn't going to be too happy when he checks his voicemail and finds a break-up message from the actress on his favorite show."

I nearly choked on my mouthful of liquid snickerdoodle. A break-up voicemail from a celebrity before seven a.m. on Thanksgiving? Diabolical.

I loved it.

Killian and I squeezed in a few more sips before passing our drinks back to Nora and Leighton. While they took off to find a spot along the race route, my future brother-in-law—because something told me that he would be putting a ring on my sister's finger any day now—and I took our places at the starting line.

"Hot damn! Is that my favorite coworker?"

Every muscle in my body tightened quicker than you could say "Thanksgiving." So much for the last twenty minutes of stretching. Bile pooled in the back of my throat, and it had nothing to do with my few sips of cookie latte.

I pasted on a smile and turned toward the smarmy voice I knew all too well. "Geoffrey," I managed through gritted teeth, swallowing past the urge to call him by his real name, *Ge-offer-y*. "Fancy meeting you here."

He grinned back at me, his white teeth on full display. They were a stark contrast to his caramel skin and chocolate-brown hair tied back in his signature low ponytail. If the spelling of his name and family connections weren't enough to piss me off, his luscious locks would do it. The dude had hair that rivaled L'Oréal models.

"I had no idea you ran," he said.

"Mm-hm."

"We should totally train together."

"Yeah, maybe." When hell froze over, and even then, there was a good chance I might strangle him with my scarf.

"I just crushed my first half-marathon in June, so I could totally give you some tips."

"You know what, Geoffrey—"

A whistle sounded before I could launch into my rebuttal. *Tips my ass.* I had two marathons under my belt from this year alone, but

I didn't have to brag about them. Whereas most people traveled for business or pleasure, I traveled to run. Just last month, I had taken a weekend trip to Chicago for the 10k Hot Chocolate Run. Nothing motivated me more than chocolate.

"Oh, look." Killian wrapped an arm around my shoulders, gently twisting me back toward the road ahead. "We're running. Cheers, mate."

My hands clenched at my sides. It only took a second or two for my brain to catch up with my mouth, just long enough for Geoffrey to take off, nearly whipping me with the ponytail spilling over his shoulder.

"See you at the finish line, Nellie Belly."

The way I wanted to wipe that smug smile off his stupid face ... but I was going to have to catch up to him first.

My feet pounded against the pavement. There was no way I would let this dickweed nepo baby get the best of me—not in the office and *definitely* not on my own turf. I knew this route better than anybody. I had been running the loop down Ocean and around 3rd Street Promenade for almost a year now.

"Don't do it, Nell," Killian urged, quickly matching my pace.

"Don't do what?"

"Whatever you're thinking." He narrowed his gaze. "Your sister gets the same devious glint in her eyes when she's up to no good."

I chewed on my lower lip and lasered in on the ponytail swishing a few people ahead of me. "Don't worry about it," I told him. "And don't hurt yourself trying to keep up. Leighton won't be happy."

His halfhearted protest fell on deaf ears as I sped ahead, chasing after Geoffrey. Killian's soccer career had come to a premature close a few years back after he'd suffered a blow to the knee. He still stayed in good shape, mostly by swimming laps, but anything beyond a light jog would be too much for him.

But not for me.

It only took half a mile for me to catch up to Geoffrey, and then another to fly past him with ease. As I rounded the second mile marker, I couldn't resist shooting a toothy grin over my shoulder toward the man huffing and puffing behind me. It was petty and childish, but that didn't make the surprised look on his face any less satisfying.

And even though I knew it was overkill and I would probably regret it later, I twisted my body to one side until it looked like I was straddling an invisible horse and shouted, "See you at the finish line, *Ge-offer-y.*"

In a split second, his expression shifted from shock and awe to blatant fear, eyes widening when he spotted something—or some-one—ahead of me. They were the last things I saw before I barreled headfirst into a blur of red-and-white velvet.

Austin

Sweet Christmas, I killed my hot neighbor.

It was the first thing that crossed my mind, followed quickly by a much more inappropriate thought about how I would never get the opportunity to see her naked. That was the real tragedy.

Not to sound too much like my older sisters, but I had been crushing hard on Janelle Wheatley—or Nellie, to her friends and family—since she'd moved into the apartment across from mine. Which made today's incident all the more embarrassing.

I had already blown any shot I had with her earlier this year when she'd asked me out to dinner. The invitation had taken me by surprise, and as any of my family, friends, or former partners would attest to, I did not do well with surprises—good or bad. And like the *cotton-headed ninny muggins* I was, I had come up with some half-baked excuse about bathing my cats and scampered back to my apartment. I had spent the next few months avoiding her at every turn, fearing I might revert to my awkward, bumbling self if she so much as smiled at me.

There would be no coming back after today's blunder, I feared.

"Excuse me," I said to the nearest person in scrubs. I didn't recognize them from the usual Thursday rotation. Then again, I usually stuck to the pediatric ward. "Can you point me toward room 274?"

"Take a right at the end of the hall. Second door on the left."

"Thank you."

"No worries." Their lips kicked up to one side before they added, "Santa."

I rolled my eyes and zipped down the hallway, bypassing the hospital gift shop. A thirty-dollar teddy bear wouldn't make up for (literally) knocking Nellie off her feet. It was going to take a lot more than that.

I had completely forgotten about the annual Turkey Trot when I'd rounded the corner of Ocean Avenue and Pacific. What should have been a shortcut to my favorite coffee shop had turned into an hour of waiting for the paramedics, surrounded by sweaty strangers dressed like turkeys and pilgrims.

As the lone Santa in the crowd, I had stuck out like a sore thumb. It was my worst nightmare—people pointing and whispering, eyeing me with disdain. And who could blame them? Someone's grandmother might have gotten run over by a reindeer at one point in time, or so the song went, but today would go down in infamy as the day some poor jogger got railroaded by Santa.

On an electric scooter.

What could I say? Parking was expensive in L.A.

I hefted the bag of toys up on my shoulder and trudged down the hall, boots clomping across the checkered linoleum floor. There hadn't been any reason to change, not when I was expected in the children's ward for "Storytime with Santa" at ten. Hopefully, Nellie would understand, or at the very least be able to forgive me.

Voices filtered out of her room before I even turned the corner.

"Please stop coddling me, Leigh Leigh." There was no mistaking Nellie's soft, melodic tone, even tinged with annoyance. It wrapped around my heart, tugging me two steps closer. "I promise, I'm fine."

"You fractured two bones in your foot, Nell. That's not fine."

Fuck. The one time I'd taken a shortcut. Nellie was laid up in the hospital with a fractured foot, meanwhile I had walked away—well, scooted away—without a scrape. Sometimes, it paid to be on the fluffier side.

I anchored my neck around the door jamb, stomach sinking when I saw her propped up by five or so pillows in a hospital bed, still clad in her cropped sweatshirt and spandex shorts. The skimpy bottoms gave way to two shapely legs that I had spent more than a few hours dreaming about wrapped around my waist—or head. I wasn't picky.

What could I say? I had a thing for women—and men, for that matter—who did living room yoga and pranced around the kitchen in their underwear.

"I still think I could have finished the race," Nellie grumbled, pouting her bubblegum-pink lips. I bit back a smile. *Of course,* that was what she was most upset about. "And don't you dare call Mom."

"Too late," her sister, Leighton, answered from beside the bed. I had never officially met the curvy brunette, but from what I had heard, she was something of an up-and-coming fashion designer.

"Great," Nellie said begrudgingly. "I swear, if she hops on a plane and shows up at my apartment, I'm telling her you're pregnant."

"Please don't even joke about something like that."

"Then please, get me out of here." She rested her manicured hands atop her flat stomach. "I'm going to be pissed if I miss out on Bowie's dinner."

"Er, can I help you, Santa?" I nearly jumped out of my boots when a hand tapped my shoulder. I turned toward the familiar British lilt, coming face-to-face with a blond-haired giant whose bushy beard rivaled my own. "Or do you prefer St. Nick?" he hedged, arching a brow.

Had we never spoken before, I might have thought he was Thor, or at the very least, the guy who played Thor on Hollywood Boulevard. But Killian and I had exchanged pleasantries in the courtyard that divided my and Nellie's apartment on more than one occasion.

"Uh, yeah." I removed my velvet hat and polyester beard, fluffing out my natural brown facial hair beneath. "It's Austin, actually. We've met before—"

"I remember. You're Nellie's neighbor. The photographer, right?" He extended his hand.

I smiled and took it. "That's right."

"And Santa Claus, apparently."

My cheeks flushed. "Yeah, about that . . . I—"

"*You.*" I spun on my heels. Nellie's eyes narrowed with recognition, piercing through my thick layer of velvet as well as the cotton T-shirt beneath. "*You're* the one who ran me down?"

I swallowed my fear and stepped into her room, dropping my bag at the foot of her bed. Killian followed, looming just over my shoulder. I might have had a couple of inches on his six-foot-two frame, but there wasn't a doubt in my mind that the athletic Brit could wipe the floor with me if he so chose.

"I did, and I cannot begin to tell you how sorry I am. It's no excuse, but I wasn't looking where I was going, and I took the turn too fast."

"To be fair," Leighton said, spinning to face her sister. "You weren't watching where you were going either."

Nellie's mouth dropped open. "Yes, I was."

"Was not. You were too busy showing off for your coworker."

"I resent that," she protested. "I was *gloating*. That ponytailed weasel isn't worth showing off for."

Leighton gestured to Nellie's right foot. Her running shoe and sock had been replaced with a tightly wound bandage. Barbie-pink toenails peeked out of the wrap. "Was it worth the fractured foot?"

Nellie huffed a heavy sigh. She was cute when she was annoyed. *Who am I kidding?* She was fucking gorgeous twenty-four seven.

And because I had never been good at keeping my big Italian mouth closed during awkward silences, I gestured to her swollen foot and said, "That looks bad."

Nellie twisted her lips. "Well, it feels worse."

"Wait, why do you look familiar?" Leighton asked, eyes bouncing between her sister and me. "Do you two know each other?"

"Austin Amato." I held my hand out to her, white fur-lined glove and all. "I'm—"

"My neighbor," Nellie finished.

She and Leighton exchanged a look, one that said so much without either of them saying a word at all. It was a technique I was all too familiar with. As the younger brother of three sisters, I had been the subject of many secret, silent discussions during my youth.

"Ohhh," Leighton drawled, understanding dawning on her face. I didn't know whether to be flattered or frightened that she had told her sister about me. "*Austin.* I love your gloves."

"Er, thanks."

"You didn't have to come to the hospital," Nellie said, evening her tone. "I know it was an accident."

I rolled the hat and beard over in my hands. "I was already on my way here when . . ."

I gestured toward her elevated ankle.

"I visit the children's wing every other Thursday and play the hospital's Santa during the holidays. Hence the bag of toys."

Her expression softened when her eyes landed on the oversized bag by my feet. "There are toys in there right now?"

"There are."

Her lips tipped up to one side. "Well, damn. That's not fair."

"What?"

"I can't be mad at a guy delivering presents to kids with cancer."

I choked back a laugh. There was nothing funny about kids with cancer or other debilitating illnesses, but that didn't make our situation any less . . . amusing? Humiliating? Some strange combination of the two?

Story of my life.

"I do need to get to Storytime with Santa—"

She snorted. "Of course you do."

"But I wanted to make sure you were okay first."

"I'll be fine." Her eyes sparkled with unshed tears. My heart—and cock—lurched when she added, "But I appreciate you stopping by, *Austin.*"

Fuck, I loved the way she said my name, all soft and breathy. I would have been lying if I said I hadn't envisioned Nellie whispering my name—or better yet, screaming it—at least a dozen or so times since we'd met, preferably while I pounded into her or ate her gorgeous pussy. None of those fantasies had included a cold, sterile hospital room. Not that I wasn't above doing a little bit of doctor-patient roleplay . . .

"See you around, Santa."

"Right," I answered. "Please let me know if you need anything. Seriously, anything at all."

"Oh, don't worry," Nellie said, a hint of playfulness behind her words. "I know where you live."

Chapter Two

December 2nd

Nellie

I had never considered myself a "romantic" person. I wasn't a fan of cutesy couple nicknames, hand holding gave me the ick—especially on a first date—and even after a year of reading my sister's favorite romance novels, grand gestures still made me cringe.

That being said, nothing warmed my heart quite like Frank Capra's masterpiece, *It's a Wonderful Life*.

Long before the days of twenty-dollar movie tickets and Netflix subscriptions, my sister and I had spent many Saturday nights picking out tapes—that was right, tapes—at the local video store. Whereas she always gravitated toward the latest rom-com releases and I preferred a grizzly horror flick, there was always one genre we could agree on—Christmas movies.

White Christmas, Meet Me in St. Louis, Elf—basically, anything featuring Bing Crosby and/or at least one song and dance sequence that had absolutely nothing to do with the plot. But if you asked me, none of them held a candle to *It's a Wonderful Life*.

For twenty-ish Christmases, I had watched Jimmy Stewart dance himself over the edge of the school swimming pool, lasso the moon for Donna Reed, and race through the streets of Bedford Falls, shouting merry greetings to passersby. Personally, I liked to believe that there was a lost alternative ending out there somewhere—one where Mr. Potter got his ass handed to him by the rest of Bedford Falls—but even without it, the movie was damn near perfect.

Sadly, due to recent events, I had taken a wrong turn on Sunset Boulevard and had ended up in a different Jimmy Stewart movie.

Rear Window.

Stuck in my apartment with a fractured foot, I watched as the rest of my neighbors—including the sexy Santa who'd run me down—go about their lives. The only thing missing was Grace Kelly. Instead, I had Tabitha.

"Please, Tabitha," I said, wincing at the desperation in my voice. "A small fracture isn't going to stop me from coming into the office."

The intimidating woman on the other end of the video call blinked back at me. Tabitha Treger could give lessons in the art of resting bitch face. Seriously, Mona Lisa had nothing on Tabitha. She was the only senior partner at the firm with experience in both intellectual property and corporate law, and even though she was one hell of a shark, something told me that if she ever gave up her career, she could make a killing as a professional poker player.

She also scared the ever-loving reindeer shit out of me.

"Honestly, Janelle. There's no reason for you to come in." She tucked her crisp blonde bob behind her ears. "We've got everything covered around here. I can have one of the interns drop off your files later today, along with anything else you might need from your desk."

"But what about—"

"Besides, isn't it your driving foot?"

I stared down at the heavy black Aircast weighing down my right foot. Black had never been my color.

"I can always Uber."

"We'll be fine. Just go ahead and focus on your current accounts." She passed a stack of papers to somebody off screen. "Geoffrey here can handle any new leads for the next few weeks."

Over my dead—

"Nellie Belly! How's the foot?"

I lurched in my seat when his face popped into frame, sending a wave of pain shooting down my leg. He certainly had a knack for popping up at the most inopportune moments, and why did those always seem to coincide with me sans makeup?

I clenched my fists at my side and smiled. "Perfectly fine, thanks."

"That was a pretty bad fall you took."

Oh, no you don't. That pompous, ponytailed bastard wasn't going to get the best of me.

"Barely felt a thing."

"Let's see that boot, then."

"I don't think so."

"Oh, come on," he pushed. "Show me."

"Let's not," Tabitha said coldly, shooing him away from her desk. "For future reference, Geoffrey, please don't ask your coworkers to show off their feet. That's a human resources nightmare waiting to happen." She quickly tacked on, "Oh, and please reschedule our meeting with Brooks Bennett and his team."

"What? No." I'd had tomorrow's meeting with Bennett Studios on my calendar since Halloween. "Please don't change it on my account. I'll get my sister to drive me if needed."

"It's already done. His assistant called this morning, requesting that we push it out a few more weeks. Something about a broken sauna at his house in Joshua Tree."

My brows furrowed. "The address we have for him is in Malibu. Do you need me to change that?"

Her lips kicked up to one side.

With anybody else, I wouldn't have thought much of the subtle smile. With Tabitha, though, she might as well have been bouncing off the ceiling with uproarious laughter.

"That's his *other* house. Welcome to Hollywood, Janelle."

"Right." A soft knock at the door drew my attention. "I'm so sorry. There's somebody at my door. Do you mind if I grab that?"

"Please do. Actually, why don't you take the rest of the day off?"

Um, what?

I didn't take days off. Ever.

Since starting with Wilson, Treger, and Faison, I had taken exactly one half-day, and that was only because my gynecologist had refused to see patients before or after normal office hours. Nonetheless, I had still made it back by eleven a.m., a smile on my face and I.U.D. in my uterus.

"Oh, that's not necessary."

"I think it is," Tabitha said with the arch of her perfectly manicured brow. "You have thirteen days of paid leave that expires at the end of the year. It wouldn't hurt to take a day or two off, especially around the holidays. And speaking of . . ."

Oh fuck, I already knew where this was going.

"How are the plans coming along for the company holiday hoopla?"

I swallowed a sigh. In my desperate need to impress the partners, I'd volunteered to organize the end-of-quarter company outing. Not a

Christmas party, but rather a company-wide holiday hoopla—whatever the hell that meant. According to some of my coworkers, past years' events had included a yachting excursion to Catalina Island, tickets to *Wicked* at the Pantages, and a private dinner in Cinderella's Castle at Disneyland.

WTF put the extra in extravagance.

Nonetheless, they were a lot more invested in their staff's well-being than either of the firms I had interned with during law school. The bar—pun intended—had officially been set.

"I'm still throwing around a few ideas." That was a lie. I had been so focused on work lately that I had barely given the holiday shindig a second thought . . . or first one.

"Fantastic. Send me some thoughts by next week, please." *Awesome.* Well, at least I would have something to work on during my sudden, extra downtime. "In the meantime, take it easy, would you?"

"I'll do my best."

"And Janelle?"

"Hm?"

She leaned in a little closer. "Don't forget about your door."

Oh, for fuck's sake.

Taking the afternoon off might not be such a bad idea after all. I had heard about "pregnancy brain" before, but was there such a thing as "fractured foot brain?"

Tabitha ended our call, and I leapt up from my swivel chair. "Leapt" might have been a bit optimistic—hobbled was more accurate. Just the short walk from my desk to the door had me breaking out in a sweat.

I nearly missed a step when I flung open the front door, though that had less to do with my bulky boot and everything to do with the man waiting on the other side of the threshold. The one holding an oversized gift basket packed full of fluffy socks, delicious treats, and my favorite trashy magazines.

Only this time, he wasn't dressed as Santa Claus.

"Hi."

"Hi," I echoed.

"Am I interrupting anything?" His eyes skirted over my bare legs. I was suddenly very aware of just how short my plaid pajama shorts were. "Er, I can come back later, or—"

"No, you're fine. I was just working from home." The sharp bite of winter air made me shiver. It was hard to believe that in just a few short weeks, L.A. had gone from seventy to fifty-degree temperatures. "Actually, my boss all but ordered me to take the rest of the afternoon off, so your timing is perfect."

He snorted. "That's probably the first time I've ever heard that."

I got the feeling that he wanted to say something else, but he left it at that. It wasn't the first time Austin had left me wanting more. The truth was, I had spent my first few months in Santa Monica shamelessly flirting with him—in the laundry room, next to the mailboxes, across the street in the community garden. And why the hell not? The man was a snack and half—*thicc* with two c's—and had a beard made for riding. Plus, he really knew his way around a plot of eggplant.

At the time, I could have sworn that the interest was mutual, which was why I'd been so surprised—and frankly disappointed—when he'd turned me down. There'd been no more flirting after that. In fact, now that I thought about it, I had barely seen him around the complex for weeks.

Maybe it was for the best, though. He had clearly found somewhere else to . . . put his eggplant, and I'd thrown myself headfirst into work. Besides, I had never been the kind of girl who chased after a man, and I wasn't about to start now.

I wanted somebody who wanted me, who was *obsessed* with me—in an obnoxiously adorable, can't keep his hands off me, and wakes me up with coffee kind of way—and I refused to settle for anything less.

"Is that for me?" I asked, gesturing toward the basket in his arms.

"Oh, yeah." He held it out to me. "Just a few things I thought might make you feel better."

"You really didn't have to do that."

"I still feel awful about what happened."

"Seriously." I huffed. "Please stop being so nice."

We both winced at the venom in my voice. He wasn't the only one that was taken aback by my pent-up frustration, none of which should have been directed toward him. Well, maybe a little. I was still salty about not being able to finish that Turkey Trot.

Before he could turn tail and run, I held up my hand.

"I'm sorry," I told him, softening my tone. "I didn't mean to snap at you. I've just . . . been a little on edge the last few days, not that that's an excuse, but still." Understanding dawned on his face. "I just meant that you don't need to keep apologizing. As much as I hate to admit it, Leighton was right; I wasn't looking where I was going, so I'm just as much to blame for this."

He nodded. "Got it."

I could have left it at that. I could have taken the gift basket inside and cracked open a gossip rag in the tub. But that would have been too easy. Instead, I gave in to the swirl of manic thoughts racing through my head, just searching for an audience.

"Now, my boss wants me to 'take it easy' and work from home, but I can't win over Bennett Studios *and* tear down that ponytailed bastard from my living room couch, now can I?"

"Probably not."

"Then there's the office holiday spectacular thing I volunteered to plan, and my mother, who won't stop calling me about Christmas, and the worst part about all of this—"

His eyes widened. "There's more?"

"I can't even do the *one thing* that always makes me feel better when I'm stressed . . . run."

I chanced a look at his face when I finally caught my breath. *Poor guy.* He had come over to check on me and deliver, by the looks of it, a well put together care package, only to be subjected to my word vomit and ire. Some neighbor I was.

My eyes roved over the basket of goodies, quickly zeroing in on a familiar package of cookies. "Did you— Are those Tim Tams?"

"Uh, yeah."

I snatched the basket out of his hands and held it up for closer inspection.

"Those are my absolute favorites."

"I know." He smiled and tucked his meaty palms into his pockets. *The things he could do to me with those thick fingers.* I shook off the thought. Fantasizing about my neighbor filling me up with his fingers wasn't exactly appropriate for a Monday morning. "You mentioned them a couple times before."

"And you remembered?"

"I remember a lot of things."

Moisture clouded my eyes. It wasn't every day that somebody gave me a package of my favorite Australian delicacy. They weren't easy to come by in the States. Most grocery stores didn't carry them—believe me, I'd checked. "Where did you even find them?"

"A small international market in Silver Lake."

"You drove across town for me?"

He shrugged. "It's not a big deal."

That was where he was wrong. I might have been a newly minted Los Angeleno, but even I knew that driving to the east side, from the west side, for a package of goddamn cookies was as good as a marriage proposal. West siders hardly ever left West L.A., aside from the occasional weekend brunch trip or tickets to a movie premiere.

Maybe it was time I reconsider that whole grand gesture thing.

I swallowed when he crossed his arms in front of his chest, my tongue suddenly heavy. Venice Beach could keep their bodybuilders; I would take a photographer's arms wrapped around me any day of the week. Hugging me tight, lifting me up and down his coc—

"I'm sorry to hear you've been going through it," he said, interrupting my second fantasy in the span of five minutes. "Let me know if you need anything else."

"Thank you, Austin."

His pupils darkened at the sound of his own name.

"My pleasure, Janelle."

The funny thing was, I believed him. Maybe taking the afternoon off to stuff my face with Tim Tams and my pussy with my favorite dildo wasn't such a bad idea after all.

Austin

"Which one of these Santas do you think is the hottest?"

I looked up from the lens in my hand to find Sloane, my photography assistant, laser-focused on an Asian Santa in neon-red swim trunks. "I thought you were off the dating market."

I hadn't met Sloane's newest beau yet, but from what she had told me, they had made things social media official right before Thanksgiving.

"That doesn't mean I can't admire the merchandise."

I nodded my head toward the subject of her attention. "Twenty bucks says he's stuffing his shorts."

"No way. I know a monster cock when I see one."

"So do I," I said around a wink.

"You're on."

Sloane had never been able to resist a competition of any kind, really. I had once seen my five-foot-nothing assistant turned best friend drink a three-hundred-pound biker under the table, all because she'd wanted a chance to drive his motorcycle. To every bar patron's shock and awe, Sloane had challenged him and won the bet. They had both been too blitzed to take the ride, though, so instead she'd taken him for a different kind of ride as a consolation prize.

People constantly underestimated her, especially men, but after three years of working together side by side, there wasn't a doubt in my mind that she could do anything she wanted to. Plus, there was a certain kind of sick satisfaction that came with watching her hand some dude twice her size his ass.

"Trade you for the 300 mm." I held out the smaller lens. It had been good for getting close-up content on the beach, but the competition was underway now, and I needed something that would clearly capture the action through the waves.

"You got it."

We made the lens switch just in time for me to capture a rainbow-bearded Santa in a jockstrap catch a ten-foot wave.

This was my second time photographing the Surfing Santa Monica competition, an annual contest that drew in dozens of surfers from across West Los Angeles as well as parts of Orange County. Per the contest rules, all surfers were required to don some kind of gay apparel, hence the beach packed full of Santas, elves, and reindeer of all shapes and sizes.

"You should learn to surf by next year so you can compete."

I shot her a lock from behind the tripod, one that said, "Sure, when reindeer fly."

"C'mon," she said, goading me. "You've already got the suit. The rest is just a board and some water."

"As easy as that?"

"You bet."

I shook my head. "We both know I'm more of a land mammal. Remember the swan boats?"

She tilted her head back and cackled. "Boy, do I."

Sloane moonlighted as a makeup artist in her spare time, so when she'd heard that one of her regular clients was planning to propose to her partner, she'd recommended me to document the proposal, a job which I'd happily accepted. Photographing local happenings and holiday events were my passion, but private events—weddings, proposals, corporate retreats—paid the bills. Camera equipment wasn't cheap.

Little had I known that the proposal would take place in a swan boat on Echo Park Lake. I'd capsized halfway through and I'd had to abandon . . . swan.

I'd still gotten the shot, though. And Sloane's client had gotten the girl.

"By the way," I said, changing the subject. "I talked to my neighbor again."

"The cute one you ran down?"

"That's the one." I had given her a bare bones account of what had happened on Thanksgiving during the Ho-Ho-Hot Dog Eating Competition we'd photographed this weekend. "I brought over an apology care package with some tea, magazines, and comfort snacks."

"Well, that was sweet of you." She twisted her lips. "I don't know why you haven't asked her out yet. It's clear that you're hard up for her."

Hard was an understatement.

"We don't really talk much." I hesitated before reluctantly adding, "Anymore."

"Anymore?"

I zoomed in on the next surfer, a woman old enough to be my grandmother decked out head-to-toe in full icy-blue body paint. A pair of snowflake nipple pasties completed her Jack Frost-inspired look.

Hang ten, Granny Frost.

"I'm waiting, Texas."

I rolled my eyes. *Smartass.* Sloane insisted on her silly nickname for me, despite knowing that I—an Italian, bisexual boy from Cleveland—had never set foot in the Lone Star State. My parents, though, in their infinite corniness, had named my sisters and I after the cities we'd been conceived in—Charlotte, Savannah, Madison, and Austin. Talk about a fun and uncomfortable factoid to learn as a child.

"She might have . . . asked me out earlier this year."

Intrigue colored her eyes. "And?"

"And I might have . . . turned her down." She tilted her head to one side and blinked back at me. "Don't look at me like that. You've seen her. She's so . . ." I bit down on my bottom lip, thinking about the brilliant beauty who lived across the courtyard. "And I'm so . . ."

"Wow," Sloane drawled. "That explains it."

"C'mon, you know exactly what I'm saying."

"What you're saying is a pretty girl asked you out and you were too scared to say yes."

Fuck yes, I was scared, and rightfully so. I was a grad school dropout turned photographer; Nellie was a lawyer, who worked hard and played harder. In the eleven-ish months since she'd moved in, I had seen her come and go—to club and bar openings, to red-carpet events, on dates with men who wore watches that cost more than my most expensive camera. Clearly, she was interested in somebody to wine and dine her, and I was more of a cocoa and cuddle kind of guy. My social battery didn't allow for much outside of work and the occasional movie night with Sloane, and I was fine with that.

A lot of my previous partners hadn't been, though, and I refused to be the one that dimmed Nellie's light.

"It doesn't matter," I told her. "Let's get some shots from the left."

She didn't let up as we made our way across the beach to get another angle. "Texas, when are you going to realize that you're the prize? Seriously, any girl, gay, or they would be lucky to call you daddy."

Sloane giggled when I tripped over my feet, catching myself—and my camera—before I nose-dived into the sand.

Never in my thirty-four years had I thought of myself as a "prize," something to be won. Not when there were so many better, younger, and more successful options. Then again, growing up as the "baby brother" to the famous Amato sisters—or infamous, depending on who you asked in Cleveland—hadn't left many opportunities to come in first, so to speak. Each one of my sisters was a powerhouse to be reckoned with, and together, they were unstoppable.

Sloane had been right about one thing, though: I was a kinky fucker. There wasn't much I wasn't up for in the bedroom, so long as it got my partner off, preferably more than once.

The things I wanted to do to Nellie Wheatley . . . fuck.

That didn't mean I talked about them out loud with anybody, not even my best friend.

"Can we not talk about her anymore?"

Sloane exhaled exaggeratedly and tucked one of her long black curls behind her ear, exposing her multiple piercings. Seeing as how she had posed for me in a series of nudes last year, I knew firsthand that there were a lot more silver hoops and balls going on underneath her demure outfit. She might put off the appearance of the girl next door, but there was a lot more to Sloane than met the eye.

"Fine." She huffed. "I'll leave it alone." She waited approximately zero-point-two seconds before quickly adding, "*But,* can I just say one more thing?"

A loud belly laugh escaped me. We both knew her too well. Not only did she always have to have the last word, but she also never shied away from telling you *exactly* how she felt. It was the quality I envied most about her.

"Don't close that door too soon, babe. I've seen the way you look at her, like she's the last slice of pumpkin pie at Thanksgiving dinner."

"I'm more of a pecan guy."

Sloane rolled her eyes. "Then you're dumber than I thought. All I'm saying is there's clearly something there. She asked you out, and you brought her snacks and apologized. Sounds like a match made in millennial heaven to me."

If snacks and a kind word or two were all it took to impress a woman these days, then heterosexual men were failing miserably.

"It sounds like you're dating the wrong men."

"You're probably right," she said, shrugging her shoulders. "I have high hopes for this new one, though." Just then, a Grinch dressed in a candy cane striped Speedo sped past us on a unicycle, surfboard strapped to his back. "Then again, if things don't work out, it looks like I have options."

Deep down, I knew what Sloane was saying made sense. Not about the Grinch—I would sooner go down in a swan boat than go down on a man covered in green fur, no matter how hung he was. By all accounts, I had a lot of great things going for me—a family who loved me (even if they didn't always understand me), a career that I loved and made a decent living at, and a rent-controlled apartment, which in West L.A., might as well have been liquid gold.

But unlike a lot of the people I had met, dated, and worked with since moving here nearly a decade ago, I didn't trade in accomplishments. Transactional relationships were a dime a dozen in Hollywood, and while that might have worked for some people, I wasn't one of them.

I didn't need a sensational or extraordinary love; comfortably quiet would do. And to be fair, there was something extraordinary about that unto itself. It wasn't every day that you found somebody you could lie with in comfortable silence for hours on end without feeling uneasy.

"Allow me to propose a toast, then," I said. Sloane cocked her head to one side and gestured toward her empty hand.

"Um, I think we're missing something. If you want to ditch this Santa fest for drinks, though—"

"Shut up and lift a lens, will you?"

I held my camera out in front of me, pointing the lens toward the clear blue sky. Sloane's eyes sparkled with intrigue. To her credit, though, she didn't question me or my sudden proclamation. Instead, she reached into my hefty equipment bag and lifted a macro lens with gusto, holding it up in front of her face.

"To taking a chance on ourselves." She lifted a brow. "And the people lucky enough to know us, fuck us, and, maybe one day, love us."

"Lucky bastards."

My attention caught on something behind her. "Speaking of lucky bastards." I pointed over her shoulder, toward the Santa currently tugging a pair of balled-up socks out of his swim trunks. "I believe you owe me twenty bucks."

"Oh, for fuck's sake."

Chapter Three

December 6th

Nellie

"Sir, please take your hands off my wiener."

I turned my face into Leighton's shoulder, trying desperately to contain the burst of laughter threatening to escape. It wasn't every day that your semi-famous friend scolded a stranger for manhandling her dog.

The man beside us held his hands up in front of him. "I just wanted to pet him."

"*Her*," Nora corrected. "And she doesn't appreciate strange men touching her."

"Me neither," Leighton and I echoed in unison. Apparently, all three of us—well, four including Banger—were in our feminine rage era.

Banger, aka Nora and Bowie's short-haired Dachshund, was equal parts princess and menace, a vengeful bitch packaged into ten pounds of black and tan adorableness. She didn't take kindly to strangers, especially men with facial hair, so it had come as no surprise to any of us when she'd snarled at Kirkland brand Colonel Sanders here for trying to pick her up—without asking first, no less. I wasn't even a pet owner, and even I knew better than that.

"*Bitches,*" the colonel muttered under his breath.

"That's right," I said without missing a beat. "Just call us the Bitches of Brentwood. And as the nastiest bitch in the coven, I can tell you two things: one, this boot on my leg can wield a lot of damage, and two, I know every legal loophole in the California code. So, what's it going to be?"

We must have looked comical to any passersby. Me, decked out in my new holly-patterned jumpsuit and Aircast, standing toe to toe with a wannabe extra from *Duck Dynasty*. Outside of a pet supply store, no less. Nora, fresh from a photoshoot, looking like she'd just stepped off the pages of *Vogue*. And Leighton, who must have been on the tail end of her period, because she was practically dressed for bed—baggy, oversized sweatpants, one of Killian's shirts, and a ratty pair of flip flops.

He swallowed and then said, "Whatever," before backing away.

Nora waited until he was nearly out of earshot before shouting, "Merry Christmas, asshole." The three of us ducked into the shop and made a beeline for the back counter. "Seriously, who the fuck tries to pick somebody else's dog up without asking? I should have let her maul his face off."

"I don't know," Leighton said, mulling over Nora's words. "Ankles, maybe, but face? She's an awfully small dog."

"Tell that to my favorite pair of boots."

Long before Nora had come along, Banger had been the love of Bowie's life, so it was no surprise that it had taken her a while to get used to the idea of another woman warming her owner's bed. Two years and at least one pair of shoes later, Nora and Banger were practically old chums.

"Aw, we should have gotten her a sweater to wear," Leighton cooed, skipping over to a display of festive clothing designed for cats and dogs. "Dang, twenty-two dollars. I could make her something for less."

"Forget it." Nora shook her head. "Bowie is very anti-clothing on animals."

"But not anti-pictures with Santa, right?" I pressed.

"Definitely not."

It had been a tough week, to say the least. Some people had been cut out for working remotely, but as I had quickly come to realize, I was not one of them. There was no hustle and bustle at home, no socializing with coworkers—even the ones who ceaselessly annoyed me. Even worse, there was no good reason to change out of your pajamas.

On top of the mindfuck that inevitably came with working from home, Bennett Studios had been playing phone tag with us all week, *and* I was still racing against the clock to come up with something for the office holiday hoopla. So, when I'd come across a social media post advertising free photos with Santa at the nearby pet supply store this weekend, I had jumped—not literally, much to my dismay—at the chance to do something, *anything*, outside the walls of my apartment.

It was either that or bang on my neighbor's door . . . or bang my neighbor. Come to think of it, maybe a good dicking was exactly what I needed.

"Careful," Leighton warned, tugging me back when I nearly tripped over a Labradoodle with antlers. "You already broke one foot this year."

"Sorry, I've just got a lot on my mind."

"Like the hot Santa that ran you over?" my sister asked, wagging her brows suggestively.

"No." Yes. "There hasn't been any time to think about him." Except every night in bed, with my vibrator cranked up to eleven. "I'm too swamped thinking about this stupid work party thing." And riding Austin's face like he was the last of Santa's reindeer.

"There's always Disneyland," Leighton suggested.

"They did that, like, two years ago."

"What about a *Top Chef* kind of thing?" Nora asked. There was only one couple ahead of us in line, plus their adorable gray pit bull. It wouldn't take long for us to see Santa. Not that I was in a rush to get out of here and back to my six hundred square feet of torture. "You know, like a tasting menu or something at a swanky restaurant. There are plenty of those to go around in L.A."

"That might work. Whatever happened to the simple stuff like caroling and decorating gingerbread houses?"

Nora shrugged. "Late-stage capitalism."

"I knew I liked you, Nora."

As it turned out, I wasn't the only one struggling to come up with a seasonal surprise. Leighton had no clue what to get Killian, and understandably so—the guy was loaded. He had everything he needed, more than he wanted, and unlike most folks, rich or not, he hardly ever asked for anything.

"Honestly, Leigh," I told her. "I'm pretty sure you could wrap yourself up naked with a red bow and Killian would be happy."

Her small smile and rosy cheeks told me that she probably already had.

"What about Mom and Dad?"

I stared back at her, puzzled by the abrupt subject change. "By all means, *please* give Killian our parents."

"No, I meant what are we going to get them?"

"Beats me," I said, answering honestly. "I haven't even begun to think about Christmas gifts yet."

"Next, please."

There was no more time to talk about gifts and parties after that. The three of us stepped forward with Banger in tow. I had to give the pet store credit; they had done a hell of a job transforming the small space into Santa's workshop, complete with staff dressed as elves, toys—of the rawhide and squeaky variety, that is—and of course, Santa.

And what a Santa he was. It was official. My libido had run rampant. I was lusting after a fictional toymaker. A tall, thick, and tattooed toymaker with chocolate-brown eyes and—

Wait a second.

"Austin?"

Santa's eyes flared. "Janelle."

Leighton pointed over her shoulder and whispered, "Santa?"

"Boss?"

That last one had come from what could only be described as the goth elf behind the camera. Her nails had been painted to match her jet-black hair and lipstick. She might as well have had "don't fuck with me" tattooed across her face.

I liked her already.

"I think I finally understand that déjà vu feeling my Aunt Millie used to always talk about."

Austin blinked.

"Babe, I think that was just her third cocktail talking," my sister said, wrapping her arm around my shoulders.

The dark elf snorted. Nora and Austin both laughed. My life had officially become a comedy of errors, only this time, everybody was laughing at me.

"So, you do this Santa thing a lot, then?"

"When I can." He gestured toward the elf behind the camera. "Sloane is my assistant photographer, and we both adopted our cats from this store, so—"

"You have a cat?"

"Three."

It was official: the man knew his way around pussy.

"As much as I would love to hear all about your cats, Santa," Nora interrupted. "I've got one disgruntled wiener dog here, and I would really love to get her home before her dad gets home from work since these photos are supposed to be a surprise."

"Of course," he said, snapping into action. He bent down on one knee and held his palm up to Banger for inspection. "And who's this?"

"This is Banger, but just so you know, she's a little skittish around strangers. Especially men. *Especially* men with facial hair, so—"

Banger was licking his hand before Nora finished. *Me too, girl.* Great, I was jealous of a dog. Within seconds, she had all but clawed her way up Austin's red suit, nestling her head into the crook of his neck.

"I'll take it from here, ladies."

The three of us watched in awe as Sloane snapped photo after photo of Austin and Banger, including at least a dozen with Banger's nose peeking out from beneath Austin's fluffy white beard.

Austin was a walking wet dream. He was *my* wet dream, at least—the proof was on my flannel sheets.

I nearly melted into the floor when his eyes shifted away from the camera and found mine. My thighs clenched when his tongue darted out to moisten his lips. They rubbed together when he narrowed his brows, almost as if he knew what he was doing to me, the power that he held over me and my body. I had never been one to relinquish control easily, but in the bedroom . . . that was a different story.

Overthinking had always been my biggest foe, one that usually got the better of me—and my orgasms—during sex, which was why I needed a partner to direct me, to move me how he liked. To orchestrate my body like his most treasured instrument.

With those sturdy arms and massive tree trunk thighs, I had no doubt that Austin could move me, throw me, and spank me however he liked, and yeah . . . that was a massive turn-on.

"Is this you *not* thinking about the hot Santa that ran you over?"

I looked over at Leighton. "I have no idea what you're talking about."

She pointed toward the corner of her lips. "You've got a little drool right there." You would have thought that after twentysomething years of her teasing, I should know better. Nonetheless, I frantically wiped my mouth.

"Did you want to get in the photo, too?" Sloane asked.

I waved her off. "No, I don't think—"

"Sure!" Nora answered for all three of us. She took up the spot on Austin's left, closest to Banger. At the same time, Leighton practically shoved me into his right side before leaning in beside me.

I tried to smile. Really, I did. I tried not to notice the warmth emanating from his body or his spicy musk that reminded me of apples soaked in cinnamon whiskey. I tried to ignore the way my body responded to him, pretending that it was just a fluke and that he wasn't the only person who had made me want like this in over a year.

"What do you want for Christmas, Janelle?"

I tilted my face down toward his. "First of all, it's Nellie. Second, are we really doing this?"

"Why not?"

"You're not expecting me to sit on your lap, right?"

"Only if you want to." *If you only knew, Santa.* "You've sat on Santa's lap before, haven't you?"

I shrugged. "Maybe once when I was a kid. At a mall."

A pang of nostalgia hit me square in the solar plexus. It had been years since I'd stepped foot in a mall—even longer since I'd visited a food court—and yet, the smell of warm pretzels and cinnamon rolls was permanently etched in my brain.

"Oh my god!" Leighton shouted, alarming all of us but especially Banger. She barked wildly in Nora's arms. "Nell, that's it."

"What?"

"We should recreate old photos of the two of us for Mom and Dad's Christmas gift."

"But—"

"Starting now with Santa."

She pushed me down onto Austin's knee before I had a chance to protest. I gasped when my clit connected with hard, thick thigh. Thank goodness he was wearing crushed velvet. The more layers between him and my weeping pussy, the better.

"You don't mind, Austin, right?"

He cleared his throat. "Oh, uh, not at all." Was it me, or had his voice dropped an octave?

"I can see that picture with the mall Santa so clearly. Okay, Nell, lean back and just straddle Austin's knee a little bit more."

Sweet. Lord.

I was going to kill her for this.

"Yes, just like that. And then, Austin, wrap your arm around her and rest your hand on her stomach."

He lifted his palm and then stopped, hesitating. "Is this okay?" he asked softly. "You can tell me if—"

"You're fine." I couldn't bear to look him in the eyes, not when my cheeks were no doubt flushed redder than Rudolph's nose. Instead, I felt for his hand and circled it around my middle. *Dear lord, his palm covers my entire stomach.* "There." He was suddenly quiet. "Does that work for you?"

"Yeah," he grumbled. "That works."

"Okay, I'm going to squeeze in next to Austin."

The moment Leighton crossed her arms over her chest and leaned back against Austin, the memory hit me all at once. I could see the photo she was talking about, the one that she had framed with popsicle sticks in first or second grade and which Mom still hung on the tree to this very day.

"Smile," Nora reminded us, snapping a photo on her cellphone while Sloane continued clicking away on her camera.

The fingers on my stomach twitched, gently toying with one of the embroidered holly berries. And then, because I was a glutton for punishment—but only if Austin did the punishing—I wiggled my core against his thigh, gasping when the movement sent shockwaves ratcheting through my clit, all ten thousand nerve endings firing at once. His entire body clenched when I did it a second time.

"*Janelle,*" he whispered against my neck. I shivered when those thick fingers dipped a little lower, inching closer to my pulsing center. "You wouldn't want me to put you on the naughty list, would you?"

The sudden flash of Sloane's camera had me jolting up and out of Austin's lap. "We've really taken up more than enough of your time,"

I told them, fumbling for excuses. "You still have a lot of pussy— I mean, *cats* and dogs to get to."

Austin blinked back at me, torn between amusement and, dare I say, disappointment?

What the fuck had I been thinking, grinding on a pet store Santa like that? My neighbor, of all people. And as I hustled Nora and Leighton out of the pet store as quickly as my Aircast would allow, all I could do was think about his question.

"You wouldn't want me to put you on the naughty list, would you?"

It wasn't the question that worried me, nor the rough timbre of his voice. No, what concerned me most was my answer.

An emphatic and resounding *fuck yes.*

Austin

Everybody grew up with *that* family. The one that wore color-coordinated, semiformal wear to Christmas Eve dinner and sent out holiday cards with an essay attached, detailing every single accomplishment of each family member from the past year. They preferred store-bought Christmas cookies over homemade—for efficiency, of course—and created a laminated set of rules for the annual gift exchange game. For them, Christmas was a show, another opportunity to broadcast their success to neighbors, colleagues, and whoever else was unlucky enough to follow them on Facebook.

Well, *that* family was *my* family.

Which was reason #82491 why I dreaded going home for the holidays.

"There's a flight out of LAX at seven a.m. Four-and-a-half hours of flight time, plus the time change . . . that should get you to Cleveland right around two-thirty p.m. That leaves exactly thirty minutes to grab your bag and make it home in time for dinner."

Spoken like a CPA.

I topped off my second cup of coffee. It was going on six o'clock, but I had a long night of editing ahead of me. Besides, I was going to need the extra caffeine boost to keep up with my sister's Christmas math.

"Char, slow down."

"This is serious. This is my first year hosting the family for Christmas, so I can't screw it up."

For some reason unbeknownst to the rest of us, our mother had decided to step down from her role as holiday hostess and pass the torch, so to speak, to Charlotte. She was the eldest Amato sibling and the only one of us—aside from our parents—who still lived in Cleveland, so it made sense in theory. Judging by her frantic tone, however, it was not the Christmas surprise Char had been hoping for.

"Here's an idea," I said. "We don't have to have dinner at three."

Silence met me from the other end of the phone.

"Char?"

"I don't understand. We always have dinner at three."

"But we don't have to. Maybe this could be the year we, I don't know, switch things up a little bit."

My cock stirred when a blur of pink darted across the courtyard, toward the laundry room at the back of the building. That was all it took to get me hard these days—pink leggings or an icy-blonde ponytail. I was still reeling from our encounter at the pet store earlier today, the one that had ended with her fleeing and me coming in my hand in the storeroom next to bags of hamster pellets.

"That's not how it works and you know it, *pasticcino*."

Well, there goes my hard-on.

I loved my sisters, but they still treated me like their baby brother, the little boy they had spent years dressing up as a pirate, prince, or ruthless outlaw for their games of make-believe. It hadn't all been bad, though. Savannah had taken me for my first manicure, a self-care practice I still partook in today, Madison, who was closest to me in age and a James Beard award winning chef, had taught me all her best cooking hacks, and Charlotte had helped me put together a business plan when I'd dropped out of business school to pursue my "photography hobby" full-time.

Most importantly, all three of them had taught me how to be a fan-fucking-tastic boyfriend . . . assuming I didn't let my insecurities get the best of me first. Spoiler alert, they usually did.

I rested my hips against the kitchen counter. "We already don't celebrate Christmas *on* Christmas, so does it really matter?"

That was another Amato family tradition—celebrating Christmas in January. Mostly because of cheaper flight prices.

"Just like Jesus would have wanted," as our mother liked to say.

"Just book the seven a.m. flight on the ninth, would you?"

"You got it, Char."

"Unless you need me to do it for you." This was exactly the kind of thing I was talking about. "I can loan you the money if you—"

"Char, I said I would book it and I will."

I could feel the weight of her judgmental stare two thousand miles away. Char might be a whiz with numbers, but she could have just as easily gone into the FBI. Her interrogation skills were unmatched.

"Fine," she grumbled.

"Looking forward to seeing you, sis."

"Uh-huh."

We said our goodbyes after that. I had just finished setting my mug down on my desk when there was a soft knock at the door. Buddy, my orange tabby, jumped down from his usual spot in the front win-dowsill to greet our visitor.

"Not a chance, Bud," I told him, scooping him up in my arms before opening the door wide for the angel in pink on the other side. "Twice in one day. To what do I owe the pleasure?"

She smiled. "Nice cat."

"He is, actually. A lot nicer than his sister, Marley." I stepped back, pointing toward Buddy's striped sibling. "Ralphie's around here somewhere, too, and believe me, you'll know him when you see him."

"Marley and Ralphie?"

"And Buddy," I said, scratching him behind the ears. His thun-derous purrs vibrated against my hand. "They all came from the same litter. Named after Christmas movie characters."

Nellie crossed her arms over her chest. She had traded in her earlier jumpsuit for something more casual—pink biker shorts and an over-sized black sweater that matched her walking boot.

"Are you sure you're not actually Santa?"

"Nah, just a chubby guy with a beard who likes Christmas." Her shoulders shook with laughter. "Did you . . . want to come in?"

I mentally cursed myself for stuttering. Just hours ago, I had all but invited this woman to grind out an orgasm on my leg. But the hat and suit were long gone, and with them my confidence, too. I wondered if superheroes experienced an identity crisis when the spandex came off.

"Sure."

I stepped back, allowing her plenty of space.

Nellie Wheatley is in my apartment. Nellie Wheatley is in my apartment.

My inner monologue made me sound like a teenage girl mooning over her first crush. *Grown men don't get crushes.* Who was I kidding?

Yes, we did. And my crush on Nellie hadn't waned, even after I'd started avoiding her.

"Wow, I wasn't expecting this."

"Expecting what?"

She gestured toward the open concept living space that mirrored her own. "You really do love Christmas."

Correction: I loved Christmas on *my* terms.

That meant anything that I knew my family would hate—a pre-lit, flocked purple tree, strand after strand of twinkling lights that looked like cowboy boots strung from ceiling to floor across the length of the living room, and, of course, the Santas.

All one hundred and twenty-two of them.

Some were antiques, picked over from estate sales and the Rose Bowl Flea Market, while others had been given to me as gifts by friends and clients over the years. There were hand-carved Santas, glass-blown Santas, and even a couple of 3D-printed Santas—all of them unique, with their own story to tell, and proudly displayed on the bookshelf beside my sofa. It was tacky to the nth degree, and I loved every bit of it.

"You haven't decorated the outside of your apartment."

"I don't decorate outside," I said, answering the question baked into her statement.

"Why not?"

"Because I decorate for me. I don't spend much time sitting outside, staring at my apartment."

Her lips twitched. "But what will the neighbors think?"

In an uncharacteristically suave move—or at least, as suave as a grown man could be while holding a cat—I moved closer to her and said, "I'm really only interested in one neighbor's opinion."

Redness tickled her cheeks. "Aww, that's sweet."

"I was talking about Mrs. Lyons in 3B."

Her blush intensified.

Where else do you blush, naughty girl?

Maybe it was the fact that I had just gotten off the phone with my sister, a season ticket holder to the Guardians, or maybe it was the striped knee sock sticking over the top edge of her walking cast, but in that moment, all I could think about was baseball. Unless the rules had changed, I should have already been out of the game.

Turning down her date invite. *Strike one.*

Spending the next few months avoiding her. *Strike two.*

Breaking her foot. *Strike three.*

All the stats pointed to another strikeout, and yet here she was, in my apartment, petting my cat. I guessed we were heading into extra innings.

"Can I get you a drink?" Buddy climbed down my body and took off toward his bed. "Or a cat?"

She bit her lip, hesitating. "How about a favor?"

"Anything," I said without missing a beat.

"That photo Leighton and I took with you earlier?"

I swallowed. "Yes."

"What would you say to doing a few more of those? Leighton had this idea to recreate old family photos for our parents and turn them into a calendar. And since you're a photographer—"

"Yes."

"We would pay you, of course."

"Absolutely not."

Her lashes blinked wildly. "But—"

"I'm happy to do it. Consider it penance for the leg."

"I already told you that wasn't necessary." Something on my face must have told her that this conversation was a losing battle. "Okay, but at least let me pay for the finished prints."

"Fine. Let me know when you pick out the pictures you want to recreate."

"Fine."

A few minutes later, after we set a date and time to go over ideas, I walked her back outside, waiting until she reached her front door before reaching for mine. Maybe it was overkill—this was a gated community, after all—but you never could be too careful.

"Hey," she called out, just before I shut my door.

"Yes?"

"I don't know about Mrs. Lyons, but *I* wouldn't mind looking at some Christmas lights when the blinds are open."

I tucked my hands into my pockets and rocked forward, smiling when her attention slipped below my waist. "I'll consider it."

Chapter Four

December 8th

Nellie

"What about the one on the slide?"

I swallowed my bite of scone and snatched the photo out of Leighton's outstretched hand. Damn, we were cute. *Still are.* Judging by the butterfly clips and floral-print romper, she must have been eight or nine at the time, which would have made me four or five. That explained the stuffed Barney toy beside me in the sand.

"I'm crying."

"So?" she asked without sparing a glance.

"So, I don't want to recreate a photo where I'm crying."

"You were always crying about something," she mumbled under her breath. Not quietly enough. "On second thought, I don't think I have anything to wear for that one, and you probably don't have a purple dinosaur toy lying around, right?"

"Right."

She tossed the photo into the pile of rejects. "Onto the next."

"Sorry, am I paying you to work or look at family photos?"

We both turned toward the freckle-faced ginger poised beside the display case full of homemade cakes and cookies.

If Austin was a snack and a half, Bowie was a fun-size treat—made in Britain.

Since taking over his grandmother's tea shop, Bowie had turned Althea's into a staple amongst tea lovers across Los Angeles. Until recently, when her designs had started taking off, Leighton had worked here full-time. The soft-spoken, short king would always have a special place in my heart because along with a job, he had offered my sister something else: friendship. A family, really. It was a small relief to know that long before I'd moved to L.A., Leighton had already had some family nearby.

"Actually, you're not paying me at all," Leighton said, smiling sweetly. "I volunteered."

When Bowie had mentioned that he was short-staffed for the holidays, Leighton had offered to fill in as needed. Unfortunately, one of the shifts had coincided with our arranged time to look through the box of family photos, and because we were both swamped with work, she'd insisted I just tag along. That was fine by me—there were worse things than spending the afternoon chowing down on Bowie's teacakes and crumpets.

"When you're finished pouring over"—Bowie paused, eyes widening when his they landed on a photo of a bare-assed baby Leighton waving around a wooden spoon—"baby bums and Barney, could you please clear the dishes from table three. We've got a book club coming in at two."

"Oh, that reminds me," I interrupted. "If you and Mom make me read another historical Highlander romance for book club—"

"But those are my favorites."

"I can't understand what they're saying. Not even when I read it."

Bowie chuckled. "Don't worry. My mums live sixty kilometers from Edinburgh and none of us can make out what they're saying either."

She held another photo out to me, which I covertly slipped to the side. We had been pouring over our memory boxes for going on two hours now, separating pictures into three piles—yes, no, and maybe. Thankfully, Leighton had yet to realize I had a super-secret fourth pile of my own, the "burn immediately so they never see the light of day again" pile.

"What about this one?" Leighton asked, turning a photo, first toward me and then Bowie. It was a picture of the two of us, along with our family dog, Murphy, on the porch swing at our parents' house. "Could we borrow your porch swing for a few hours, Bo?"

"And your dog?" I added.

He heaved a sigh. "This feels like a trick question. Like when Nora tells me she doesn't want anything from In-N-Out, but really she's expecting Animal Style fries."

Leighton gently smacked his chest. "Always get the fries, Bo. Always."

His lips tipped up on one side. "Fine." His blue-tipped finger jutted out, reminding me that I was desperately in need of a manicure. The Bubble Yum pink had chipped off three of my fingers. "I like the one with the two of you by the Ferris wheel."

"Me too!" I exclaimed. Some of my fondest childhood memories had come from spending spring break at our Aunt Holly's house in Ocean City, New Jersey. My first kiss had happened on that Ferris wheel.

"We can take it at the Santa Monica Pier."

"Works for me." A lightbulb went off while I polished off the last of the teacakes. "Mm, what about high tea?"

"As in cannabis and chamomile? Count me in."

"That's not what I meant."

Although, I was willing to revisit that idea at a later date. Leighton had indulged in what our grandmother referred to as the "devil's lettuce" for years, mostly to ease her PCOS, and she had finally convinced me to try it out when I'd moved to L.A. The first and only time we'd smoked together had ended with me passing out in a lawn chair in hers and Killian's backyard.

"I meant for my office holiday shindig. There's a hotel in Pasadena that does a Victorian-themed high tea event for the holidays featuring a string quartet and an appearance from Queen Victoria herself."

Or whatever actress they hired off Central Casting to play her.

"Sure," she said, drawing out the word. "That could be fun."

Uh-oh. I knew that tone. It had haunted me ever since the summer when I'd trimmed my own bangs. She might as well have said, "I told you so."

"What?"

"Nothing."

"It's not nothing. That's not your 'nothing' face."

She shrugged. "It's just a little . . ."

"Elegant?" I supplied when she trailed off. "Classy, luxurious?"

"Stiff."

"It is *not* stiff." She arched a brow. *Fuck, I hate it when she's right.* More like I hated when I was wrong. "Okay, so maybe it is, but what else would you expect for a group of corporate attorneys?"

"Lawyers still like to let loose." Her lips pinched together. "Look, whatever you decide will be fine. It doesn't have to be some expensive, stuffy affair. They probably get enough of that in their everyday lives, don't you think?"

"I guess."

She wasn't wrong. Contracts and litigation accounted for a small part of being a lawyer these days, especially in a city like L.A . Schmoozing made up for the rest. As a firm that catered to high-profile celebrity clients, we were constantly expected to represent the firm at film screenings, exhibit openings, and concerts. Just last month, I had met Hozier backstage at the Hollywood Bowl, and yes, he really was amazing—and gorgeous—in person.

Maybe I was overthinking the holiday party. Then again, it might be just the thing to set me apart from the rest of the junior associates, especially the sniveling suck-ups who were there on their daddy's dime. After the last few weeks, I needed a win.

"Okay, the Ferris wheel picture makes twelve," Leighton declared. She lifted her teacup toward the twinkle lights strung above us. "Sis, I believe we have a calendar."

"To us," I said, mirroring her action with my own cup.

"Cheers."

We slurped our tea like motherfucking ladies. Queen Victoria—the real one—would have been horrified.

Austin

This is it. This is how I die.

I was hiking the Hollywood Hills with my assistant and her latest boy toy. I had always pictured something a little more mundane and a lot less . . . true-crime podcast.

But no, this was what I got for saying yes to a surprise outing.

"Almost there," Laric shouted from at least ten yards ahead of us. "Come on, you two."

Sloane smiled. "Right behind you, babe."

The moment he rounded the curve of the path, her smile soured. She bent forward, collapsing to the ground on all fours. "Fucking hell," she whisper-shouted, careful not to alarm her new beau. "Why the fuck would anybody do this for fun?"

I dropped down beside her, leaning back against the rocky shelf as I tried to catch my breath. "Exercise gives you endorphins." *Breathe.* "Endorphins make you happy." *Wheeze.* "Happy people—"

"Don't you dare quote *Legally Blonde* to me at a time like this."

The jewel dotting her belly button glistened in the sunlight when she stripped down to her sports bra and used the discarded shirt to wipe her face. I envied Sloane's confidence. Both of us were big bitches, but she wore her stretch marks like badges of honor.

"I'm never going to forgive you for this one," I told her after I finally caught my breath. Whoever had come up with hiking deserved to die a slow and painful death, preferably while being chucked off the top of a mountain.

"That makes two of us." She waved when another hiker leapt over our outstretched legs before jogging up the trail. "C'mon, that's just showing off."

"The sex better be worth it."

Her pause told me everything I needed to know.

"It is," she eventually answered.

"Sloane—"

"It will be. We just . . . haven't found our rhythm yet."

I could tell there was more, but I didn't want to press her. To say that Sloane had a nasty habit of picking the wrong men would be an understatement. Her relationship history read like a bad soap opera.

There'd been the dog walker who enjoyed having food eaten off his dick, the therapist who had stolen some of his clients' trauma to use in his book of poetry, and worst of all, the stand-up comedian. There was a special place in Dante's seventh circle of Hell for amateur comics.

Sloane didn't have a type, other than emotionally unavailable men.

Funnily enough, Laric seemed like an okay guy, minus the intense, outdoorsy stuff, but clearly, the chemistry between them was lacking.

"He's the first good guy I've dated in like . . . forever. I *should* be grateful for that. I *should* want to strip him down and ride his face at all hours of the day."

"But you don't." It wasn't a question.

She circled her arms around her knees, drawing them back toward her chest. "Maybe there's something wrong with me."

My heart sank. In this moment, she didn't look like my badass rock star of a friend, but rather a lost, little girl searching for her place in the world. Tattoos and piercings, and in my case, a Santa Claus costume, couldn't protect you from those kinds of thoughts.

I wrapped my arm around her shoulders. "Nothing is wrong with you. No more than the rest of us, at least."

She shoved me away with a half laugh, half groan.

"Okay, enough of this personal feelings shit. Tell me more about the calendar project for your girlfriend."

"You know perfectly well she's not my girlfriend."

"*Yet.*"

"We're supposed to meet up later tonight to discuss details—locations, times, dates."

"Ah! You said dates." I rolled my eyes. "Love is in the air."

"How can you tell from this high up?"

It really was one hell of a view, even from the gravel path. There were a lot of stereotypes about Los Angeles—many of which were, unfortunately, true—but most people didn't realize just how beautiful the city was, especially from above. From here, the L.A. skyline looked like a series of building blocks, surrounded on either side by a blanket of homes and palm trees.

"Have you asked her out yet?"

"No." I shot her a cheeky grin. "Maybe there's something wrong with me, too."

"Well, at least you admit it."

"Shut up," I told her before devolving into laughter again. Every introvert had at least one emotional support extrovert in their lives, and Sloane was mine. We had a lot more in common than I thought either of us wanted to admit, too.

"Everything okay over there?"

Our heads pivoted toward the shirtless man waiting at the top of the path. *Damn, Laric could get it.* If it didn't work out between him and Sloane, I wouldn't mind giving him a go. On second thought, I would rather be alone for the rest of my life than date a hiker. Lumberjack, fine—I looked great in flannel—but someone who climbed hills for fun? Absolutely not.

"Uh, yeah," Sloane said around a smile. "We were just taking in the spectacular view from down here."

"It's a little bit better at the top of the hill." When neither of us moved, he shuffled over to Sloane's side. "On second thought," he said, planting himself on the ground beside her. "I've never seen it from down here, so what do I know?"

Hmm, maybe there was hope for Laric after all.

"Wow, you were right." He cuddled closer to Sloane, peppering the top of her sweaty head with kisses. "That is an incredible view."

He wasn't talking about the skyline.

It took me twice as long as usual to walk from the Lyft to my front door. The stiffness had already begun to settle into my thighs. So much for getting some work done tonight. I had a blind date in the bathtub with Dr. Teal.

The petite blonde balancing on a ladder outside my fenced-off patio took me by surprise. "What the hell are you doing?"

Nellie barely spared a look over her shoulder. "Decorating your house."

"I told you—"

"That you decorate for you and that you don't see your outdoor lights, I know."

My eyes homed in on the bare strip of skin above her leggings when she stretched an inch or two higher, reaching for the edge of my roof. The sun had set almost an hour ago, and yet here she was, stringing up blue, green, and purple bulbs across the eave.

"But you know what? I do." She carefully descended the ladder, the hard plastic of her cast clunking against every metal rung on her way down. When she finally reached the sidewalk, she whirled on me. "I want to look outside with my mug of hot cocoa and see pretty lights. And since you won't let me pay you for the photos—"

"It's only fair since I broke your—"

"And you insist on making up for breaking my foot, even though that wasn't your fault." She stalked closer, stopping only when we were toe to toe. "This is the least I can do."

A smile crept across my face. "Thank you. It looks perfect."

"*Almost* perfect," she said. "But it's still missing something."

She scurried over to a plastic tub brimming with decorations and bent over to reach inside. I blew out a breath and turned away to conceal my hard-on. *What a fucking creep.* Here she was, putting up holiday lights on my house like Santa's favorite elf, and I could barely contain my erection.

"This should do it."

By the time I turned back around, she was already halfway up the ladder. "Wait, you've already done enough," I told her. "Please, let me do that."

Ladders made me nervous on principle; beautiful women on ladders downright terrified me.

"I'm plenty capable, thank you. Besides, it needs to be just right."

"But your foot—"

"Is fine. You seriously need to stop treating me like I'm breakable. Besides, it's going to look great, I promise. Almost—"

I was racing across the patio before it even happened, sore muscles long forgotten. One second, she was tacking a nylon Santa to the roof shingles, and the next, she was falling backwards, hand searching for something to catch her.

And she found it.

The breath whooshed out of both of us when she landed in my arms. For a moment, we both stayed there just like that, clinging to each other and trying to catch our breath. Her nervous gaze bounced between the ladder and the hands woven tightly around my neck, just beneath my beanie. I knew she could feel my ragged pulse and that it matched her own. There was also no use hiding the erection prodding her side, not when her lush curves were pressed so close to me.

"Are you okay?" I wheezed.

She nodded.

"Did I hurt you?"

She shook her head.

"I'm going to need your words, Janelle."

She swallowed and loosened her grip. "I'm okay," she answered softly. "You can put me down now."

"Not yet."

I wasn't ready to let her go just yet, and she wasn't complaining. Eventually, I walked us over to her side of the courtyard and dropped her down into the wicker chair on her patio—her favorite reading spot. I had seen her tear through more than a few thriller novels while cozied up in that chair.

"That was . . . exciting," she said.

"That's one way to put it."

I crouched beside her, gauging her face for any sign of distress but finding none. Surprise, maybe, coupled with a hint of embarrassment, but otherwise, she seemed okay.

That makes one of us.

My heart had plummeted out of my asshole when I'd seen her teeter on that ladder. That was twice now I had watched her fall, and both times had left me breathless.

Because I couldn't imagine going to sleep tonight without touching her, without knowing that she was okay, I lightly dragged a finger across her cheek, tucking a stray piece of hair behind her ear. Nellie's doe eyes blinked up at me, silently pleading with me to say something, do something. To take the lead. *Interesting.* Something told me that Nellie wasn't used to letting go of control, and yet maybe that was exactly what she needed.

Maybe that was what I could give to her.

"Why are you all sweaty?"

"Huh?"

Her finger traced a path across my chest. "You look like you mud wrestled a mountain lion."

"I, uh, went for a hike."

Her nose scrunched up. "I hate hiking."

I reeled back with surprise. Nellie was the textbook image of athleticism. "Miss jogs five miles a day?"

"Only on flat ground."

Her eyes shot up when I captured her hand in mind, trapping it against my chest.

"I think that's enough decorating for the night," I told her.

Her eyes narrowed, lips flattening into a thin line. "But the Santa." I looked over my shoulder when she pointed at St. Nick dangling from my roof. "He's crooked."

Ironically, the decoration had been designed to look like he was hanging off the edge, but Nellie had only nailed one of his hands to the roof before her tumble. It wasn't perfect, and yet it was better.

"I don't know," I told her. "I kind of like him like that. Seems more playful and . . . messy."

"Messy?"

"Not in a bad way. I find that usually, when somebody knows they're being photographed, they get stiff. Like they're putting on a show." She squinted up at Santa while mulling over my words. "The best photos are usually candid. Fun, a little bit messy, but a beautiful mess. They tend to capture a piece of us that we often keep hidden."

"A beautiful mess," she repeated.

"But I can straighten him out, if you want me to."

"No," she said with a smile on her face. "I think I like him exactly how he is."

I had a funny feeling that she wasn't talking about Santa Claus anymore.

Chapter Five

December 11th

Nellie

I had never taken kindly to being told what to do, something both of my parents and sister would attest to—youngest child syndrome and all that. That being said, Austin could have very well ordered me to crawl to him on all fours and I would have done it. Happily.

"Okay, Nellie, lean in a little bit more." I did as he said, pushing in an extra inch until my nose brushed the tree's needles. "That's it. And tilt your face up toward me."

Our eyes met when I lifted my chin. The intensity of his gaze made me swallow. This was a different side of Austin, the same one I had seen a few nights ago when he'd saved me from what would have been another embarrassing fall. He was calm and collected, which was enough to put me on edge.

And make me wet.

"Keep your eyes on me."

Yes, sir.

Woah, where had that come from?

"My arm is falling asleep." Leighton moaned from the other side of the tree.

"Oh, be quiet. At least you have two good feet to stand on."

Meanwhile, I looked like a Christmas flamingo. My affinity for the color pink had begun at an early age, as evidenced by the photo we were recreating.

The Christmas tree lot in Culver City was our fourth and final stop of the day. In an effort to maximize our time and limit the number of filming locations, I had put together a map—with a corresponding, color-coordinated spreadsheet—for what we were now referring to as the Christmas Calendar Crusade. Three days, four photos per day, and boom, we'd have a calendar.

Leighton had done a once-over of my spreadsheet and then had looked at me like I was the Ghost of Christmas Past. Austin, on the other hand, had simply smiled and said, "Whatever you want."

You have no idea the things I want to do to you, Santa.

Or the things I wanted him to do to me. Once he got the shot, of course. We had a schedule to keep.

"Alright, cue the snow."

Somewhere behind us, Killian tossed a handful of fake snow into the air. That was the trickiest thing about recreating pictures originally taken in Ohio—no snow. Thankfully, it hadn't been hard to find a substitute in the land of movie magic, and Killian had been more than happy to help.

"We got it."

Leighton relaxed her arms and raced over to smooch Killian. Meanwhile, I let the blood return to my other leg. As it turned out, modeling was not for the faint of heart—or foot.

"Okay!" I announced once I could feel both feet again. "Let's pick out my tree."

Austin arched a brow.

"You're actually buying a tree?"

"Of course," I told him. "Did you really think we were going to visit a tree lot without taking home a tree? What kind of monster do you take me for?"

He tucked his hands into his coat pockets and bounced back and forth on the balls of his feet. That plaid wool coat was doing wonders for him. Maybe there was room for one more under there . . .

"You just struck me as more of a pre-lit, fake tree kind of girl."

Leighton and I both gasped, beyond horrified.

Killian shook his head. "Now you've done it, mate."

That was putting it lightly. Austin didn't realize the can of worms he had just opened. He was about to, though.

His eyes darted between my sister and me when we surrounded him, like a cut scene from a subpar mafia movie. "That's the worst thing you could possibly say to me," I told him. "Wheatleys don't do fake trees."

"Or tinsel," Leighton added. "Never tinsel. It's flammable."

"You're welcome to head back without us, but I am not going home without a tree. Besides, our mom would be horrified if she knew that I waited until the eleventh to get one."

Those wicked lips of his split into a smirk. "Sounds like we're picking out a tree, then."

He winked, and my panties went up in flames.

It was unnerving, feeling this way, especially about somebody I hadn't even kissed. Somebody who had turned me down and avoided me at all costs for months. But there was something about Austin—an air of mystery that I hadn't been able to solve yet—that drew me in.

And this time, I wanted more.

Leighton clapped her palms together. "I'm going to grab us all hot chocolate from the front."

"Thanks, princess," Killian said, dropping a kiss on her lips before she jetted off toward the tree lot's café. He waited until she was out of earshot before turning back to face me. "So, we need to talk."

"Aw, Killian, are you breaking up with me?"

"No." He pulled a velvet box out of his pocket and cracked it open. My hands shot up to smother my gasp when I saw the pear-shaped diamond resting inside. "I'd like to make you my sister-in-law."

"Oh my god!"

"Wow," Austin said, eyeing the massive rock. "Congratulations. That is one hell of a ring."

"Thanks, mate. Leighton actually picked it out at an antique store we visited in Carmel."

"Oh my god."

"But I had it reset with the diamond from my mother's necklace."

"Oh my god." I sniffled.

They both laughed at my expense. I couldn't be bothered to care, not when I was face-to-face with my sister's future engagement ring and the man who loved her more than life itself.

I want that.

A sudden pang in my heart made me pause. Love had never been a part of my immediate plan, at least not until I made partner. It was hard enough climbing the corporate ladder in a male-dominated field; a boyfriend would just be another distraction. Hell, I could barely keep a houseplant alive. The last thing I needed was another person to worry about.

But every now and then, I couldn't help but feel like life might be a little bit better, and a whole lot easier, with a different kind of partner.

Somebody to lie next to me at night and drink the second half of the coffee pot in the morning, to pull the laptop out of my hands when it was well past business hours and ravage me on the couch after *Dancing with the Stars* ended.

A girl could dream.

I was thrilled that my sister had found that, but I would be lying if I said I wasn't a tiny bit jealous.

Nonetheless, I threw my arms around Killian's shoulders and squeezed him tight. The big oaf towered over me, so my face ended up buried in his massive pectorals. "I'm so excited for you," I whispered against his chest. "Both of you."

When I pulled away, I snuck a glance at Austin. A wounded look crossed his face when he noticed the unshed tears in my eyes.

"Happy tears," I explained, hoping to relieve his concern. He gave a small smile in return. Why did it feel so good to know that he was worried about me? "Okay, okay, enough of that. You better put that rock away and help me find a tree before she gets back and finds us like this."

Killian tucked the ring box back into his pocket while I swiped at a runaway tear. Ring or not, Leighton would definitely know that something was up if she came back from getting hot chocolate to find tears streaming down my face, especially during one of my favorite Wheatley family traditions.

Christmas hadn't begun without a tree in our house growing up, one that we'd usually cut ourselves on a tree farm, or once, on the side of the highway. We didn't talk about *that* time because our matriarch, the esteemed Wanda Wheatley, still refused to believe that she might have broken the law.

"What about Terrence?" Killian asked as we perused an aisle of Douglas firs.

"No."

Austin's brows drew together. "Terrence who?"

"Terrence the tree," Killian said, rolling his eyes. "Leighton and Nellie's family names their trees."

"Every year?"

"That's right," I said proudly. "Why is that so weird? They're a part of the family, for a few weeks at least."

"And then they die."

"Don't say that in front of them," I scolded, gesturing toward the rows and rows of Christmas trees.

His laughter didn't deter me from the mission at hand. This was my first Christmas in an apartment of my own, in a new city, so the tree had to be perfect. And sure, I would still be spending all of Christmas Day and most likely Christmas Eve with my family at Killian and Leighton's house, but this was for me. Something to bring me joy during an otherwise stressful time of year.

"I'm sure you and your family have some weird traditions, too."

"Well, let's see," he mused. "Mom will cry at least three times, my sisters, Savannah and Madi, will fight over the last bottle of red, and at least one of my nieces will pass out at the dinner table before we make it to dessert. You've heard of the Feast of the Seven Fishes, right?"

I nodded. *I don't even think I can name seven kinds of fish.*

"In the Amato house, it's more like twelve fishes. I'm talking clams, calamari, sardines, even octopus, which isn't easy to come by in Cleveland."

I stopped in my tracks. "Wait, you're from Cleveland?"

"Uh-huh. The Mistake on the Lake."

"I'm from Plain, just outside of Columbus."

His lips twitched at the corner. "It sounds like we were always meant to be neighbors."

I refused to dignify that one with a response, instead smiling to myself while we continued perusing the tree lot. Ten minutes later, I had nearly given up on finding my tree when we came across a blue spruce.

"That's the one," I told them.

I knew it in my bones. It was . . . all wrong, and yet so incredibly beautiful. *A beautiful mess.* Austin's words had stuck with me for days. It had taken me a while to wrap my head around the idea of finding beauty in something messy, two concepts that until now had always worked in opposition, from my perspective at least. But I was starting to see what he might have been talking about.

"Really?" Killan asked, arching a brow. He had every reason to doubt my choice. It was one of the scrawnier trees on the lot, buried behind the rest. "It's a little . . ."

"Beautiful," Austin finished. We both circled the tree, eventually meeting in the middle on the opposite side. "I think it's a great choice."

"I know it's a little lumpy in the middle and bare around the top, but—"

"It's perfect."

From the corner of my eye, I saw Killian slip away. "It's not perfect," I told him.

"It is because you chose it."

Sweet baby Jesus in the manger. Take me now.

My face flamed. *This* was the Austin I had flirted with in the laundry room all those months ago. *This* was the Austin who had starred in my dreams—and more than a few wide-awake fantasies—as of late. Apparently, all it had taken was a broken foot and some Christmas lights to break him out of the protective shell he had so carefully constructed for himself.

And he was going to kiss me. He was going to kiss me now.

"Janelle," he said in a half whisper, half groan. His warm, minty breath fanned my cheeks. I planted my hands lightly on his chest and leaned up on my toes, a difficult feat when you only had one foot to work with.

And then, just as our lips barely touched—

"Okay, I just got off the phone with Nora," Leighton said.

Fate intervened. *That bitch.*

We quickly broke apart. Killian bounded over to Leighton, relieving her of the tray full of to-go cups in her hands. "Thanks, killjoy."

"What about Nora?" I asked, attempting to ignore the fact that she had just interrupted me from sucking face with the Santa next door.

"She and Bowie are going to meet us back at your place for drinks and tree decorating."

"Sounds good to me." I directed her attention toward my newly acquired blue spruce. "Meet Bruce."

She shook her head, a small laugh escaping from her lips. "Bruce the spruce? Cute."

Together, the four of us loaded the tree into the back of Killian's SUV. I had another doctor's appointment on the twentieth, but until then, I was still begrudgingly riding shotgun. A passenger princess I was not.

Pillow princess, on the other hand . . .

"Austin, you're coming back to Nellie's place to help us decorate, right?"

Austin's eyes found mine from the other side of the car, the question in them clear as day. "Only if Nellie wants me to."

"Of course I do," I said much too quickly.

His eyes lit up. My cheeks warmed when I realized how that sounded. "I mean, of course you're welcome to come."

"Then, we better get going. Bruce isn't going to decorate himself."

Austin

"Okay, who cut the cheese?"

Nellie's question was met with a few snorts and giggles.

"I beg your pardon?" Killian asked, without a trace of humor.

"Very funny," Nellie said, rolling her eyes. "Aside from Killian, you all have the humor of a twelve-year-old boy. Seriously, though, what happened to my cheddar?"

She held up a rectangle of aged cheddar cheese in one hand and a slightly smaller piece in the other. "They don't match."

Leighton snatched the larger piece and promptly nibbled the end off, trimming it down to match the other. "There, now they do."

I had decorated my fair share of gingerbread houses. In fact, as an uncle to nearly a dozen nieces and nephews, I had decorated gingerbread castles, horses, and even a spaceship or two, but Nellie and her friends had taken it to the next level by cutting out the spicy cookie altogether.

Which was why we were decorating charcuterie houses.

"Okay, full disclosure," Nora announced. "Mine isn't so much a chalet as it is . . . the cottage from *The Holiday*."

Scratch that—*charcuterie chalets*.

Nora and Bowie had met us back at Nellie's apartment nearly two hours ago, arms full of reusable shopping bags. Together, the six of us had decorated Nellie's tree, Bruce, while listening to Nora's aptly named *A Very Cute, Very Demure, Very Merry Christmas* playlist. Tree decorating had led to another round of hot chocolate—this time with peppermint schnapps—followed quickly by our current activity.

Cheese and crackers of all shapes and sizes littered Nellie's rustic white table, along with sprigs of rosemary and berries for trees and foliage, mixed nuts for a cobblestone pathway, and a wide selection of deli meats—because a house wasn't a home without a salami or two. That last bit might have come from my nona, and in my experience, Nona knew best.

"Will somebody please pass the pepperoni?" Bowie asked. "I'm going for something . . . thick and meaty."

"That's what he said," Leighton and Nora answered together before breaking out into laughter. Nellie tried—and failed—to resist the urge to join them.

It was impossible not to grin, watching them gas each other up, laugh at each other's juvenile dick jokes. They reminded me of my sisters. Well, maybe not Nellie—there was nothing brotherly about the way I felt about her, the things I wanted to do to her. Nonetheless, she had the spirit of an Amato sister. All three of them did. There wasn't a doubt in my mind that if my sisters ever joined forces with this dynamic trio, the lot of them could conquer the world. Or burn it to the ground, whatever they preferred.

"Here, you can have mine," Nellie said, forking her pile of pepperoni over to the redheaded Brit. "I wouldn't say no to extra parmesan snow, if anybody has some to spare."

Her eyes lit up when I nudged my bag across the table in her direction.

"Thanks, Santa."

My pants tightened when she bit down on her bottom lip. *Save some for me, naughty girl.* In a different cinematic universe—or maybe a cheap porno—I would have swept the artisanal crackers and sliced prosciutto over the edge of her small dining table and crushed my lips to hers. That might not have gone over well with her friends, though.

I couldn't help it. She was too tempting, too beautiful, too everything, and I wanted it all.

"Do you mind if I ask how the whole Santa thing started?"

"Not at all," I answered Killian. "It was about ten years ago. My oldest sister's husband passed away right before Christmas, and in an effort to cheer her and her twins up, I came dressed as Santa to our family's Christmas dinner. It sort of became a tradition after that, one that we still do today, even though most of the kids are teenagers."

Leighton bit into one of the crackers holding up her house. "That's so sweet."

"I kind of kept it up for fun when I moved to L.A. At first, it was just to make a few extra bucks around the holidays, but now, it really just makes me happy to make other people happy."

Nellie's lips split into a grin. "You're good at it."

"Being Santa?"

"Making people happy."

Everything else slipped away after that. Time, insecurities, our audience—gone. For now, there was only us. Only this. Her eyes locked on mine. Pools of piercing amber-brown liquid filled me with visions of things I had no business thinking about, especially not in the company of other people.

"*Bugger*, my roof is caving in."

And just like that, it was over. We were back to being neighbors and pretending that there was nothing between us, aside from some nuts and cheese.

But I knew better.

We both did.

We called it an evening when Bowie's pretzel roof caved in.

After wiping down her table and making sure that every spare slice of cheese had been carefully locked away in the fridge, Nellie walked me to the door.

"Thanks so much for today," she said while I slipped into my jacket. It was a short walk back across the courtyard, but the cold spell sweeping SoCal was no joke. Last night, I had even (gasp) turned the heater on. "I'm really looking forward to seeing the pictures."

"I can have them uploaded and emailed to you tonight."

She lifted her shoulders. "Whenever."

"Hey, you two." Nora pointed toward something above the doorway. "You know what that means."

I looked up and froze.

Mistletoe.

As if in slow motion, I lowered my eyes from the small, hanging plant to the woman standing opposite me. We had already nearly kissed once today; it couldn't hurt to give it another go. On the contrary, I might burst if I didn't finally get my mouth on hers.

I wet my lips, anxiously awaiting her next move. As much as I wanted this—wanted her—nothing would happen without her giving the go-ahead. An enthusiastic and unwavering yes. I refused to be anybody's regret, especially Nellie's.

My gaze traveled over her face, searching for any signs of distress or embarrassment but, thankfully, finding none. Instead, she gave a slight smile and lifted her hands to my shoulders, using them for leverage.

"This is the part where you kiss me, Santa," she whispered against my lips.

"Are you sure that's what you want?"

She shook her head. "It's what I need."

There was no more talking after that. I crashed my lips down on hers, swallowing up her surprised gasp.

And just like that, everything else faded away—the claps and cheers of our nearby audience, the hiss of the heater above our heads, the faint melody of a familiar Christmas song—all of that fell by the wayside as I got my first taste of my neighbor. *My naughty girl.* The woman that I had been nonstop dreaming about since that very first day we'd met in the laundry room.

When I pulled back, she followed, searching for more. And as much as I wanted to give it to her, this wasn't the time or the place. Her face fell when I carefully disentangled her arms from around my neck and stepped closer to the door.

"Thanks for a great night," I managed, my throat shaky. "I better get going." I caught her chin with my free hand and directed her to look up at my face once again. When she did, the vulnerability in her eyes made my heart jolt. "I'll talk to you soon, Janelle."

Her nod was all the response I needed.

I all but ran out the door, barely sparing a passing wave to her friends. By the time I made it to my apartment, I was burning up. My pants were unbuttoned and shoved down my thighs before the front door clicked shut. There was no time to think, only feel.

I wrapped a hand around my heavy cock, drawing it out of my boxer briefs and falling back against the door. There was no suppressing the moan that fell from my lips.

"*Fuck.*"

I hoped she heard me. I hoped they all heard me and the desperate longing behind my cries. This wouldn't take long, not with the way we had been edging each other all week.

Does she touch herself like this?

Better yet, would she let me watch? I palmed my greedy cock to the thought, grunting as I pictured her fucking herself with her fingers and, better yet, her favorite toy. *A Barbie-pink dildo with sparkles.* It had to be. Nothing else would do, not for my pint-sized elf with fuck me heels and fuck off energy.

She was in need of a good spanking, and I wanted to be the one to give it to her.

Does she think of me when she gets off?

That one nearly had me spilling in my hand.

Precum beaded the head of my cock, and I used it to lubricate my strokes, gliding my fist from tip to root, slow but firm. An image of her lying beneath me in my bed, blonde locks splayed across my pillow, flashed across my brain, fueling my need.

Her wrists were bound to the headboard, wrapped in the same golden rope that looped through my toy sack. Tears leaked from her eyes while I fed her every last inch of my cock until it scraped the back of her throat.

Fuck, I could see her, feel her so clearly.

My hand pumped furiously in time with each rapid breath. I grunted out my pleasure, the sound almost feral, like an animal craving his next meal. I knew what I was hungry for—Nellie's juicy pussy. Nothing else would satisfy this insatiable craving.

Any second now.

I pictured her small, ripe breasts bouncing with every thrust inside her mouth, every ripple of her throat around my cock driving me closer and closer to the finish line. But I wouldn't give her the satisfaction of coming in her mouth, not even if she begged for it. No, I wanted to paint her body with my cum, cover her tits, her pussy, her lips, every inch of her until she knew she was mine.

That was all it took to send me over the edge—the image of spending myself on her peachy skin and, more specifically, her lazy, satisfied grin when I did.

At this point, it wasn't a matter of *if* I made Nellie Wheatley mine, but *when*, and from the looks of it, Santa would be coming down her chimney before Christmas Eve.

My laughter echoed off the walls of my apartment. Apparently, I also had the sense of humor of a twelve-year-old boy.

Chapter Six

December 14th

Nellie

As far as I was concerned, there were two kinds of people in this world—the weirdos who believed *Die Hard* was NOT a Christmas movie and the rest of us who knew better. I could deliver a Ted Talk about my feelings on the subject and was prepared to do so at any point this evening.

Nora's friends, Devin and Riley, had invited her and Bowie to join them for a special screening of the Bruce Willis classic, and in typical third-wheeler fashion—or in this case, fifth-wheeler—I had invited myself along.

To be fair, I was in it more for the movie theater snacks. As far as I was concerned, no movie going experience was complete without a bucket of popcorn drenched in butter and salt. I even kept a miniature saltshaker in my purse at all times, just in case.

"This is gorgeous," Riley said, admiring the theater's art deco style. "Who knew this place was buried between skyscrapers?"

I nodded. It really was beautiful. Magical, some might say. Floor-to-ceiling decorative columns decked out in garland, a grand staircase leading up to the balcony seats, and a domed ceiling that would make Michelangelo weep. And that was just the lobby.

Now that I thought about it, I couldn't remember the last time I had been inside a theater, let alone gone to see a movie. Until recently, it had been months since I'd spent an evening beyond my apartment or the four half-walls of my cubicle. Yet here I was, spending another night out with friends, exploring a part of town I hadn't been to before, even after nearly a year of living in L.A.

Maybe there was something to this work-life balance thing. *God, I hate it when my sister's right.*

"Should we shop first?" Devin asked, arm entwined with their wife's. The two of them were coming up on their second wedding anniversary, and they still acted like newlyweds. "Or find seats?"

"Ooo!" Nora shouted excitedly, pointing in the direction of what looked like a life-sized snow globe. "Let's check out the photo booth."

She pulled Bowie along and the rest of us followed, carving a path through the festive moviegoers like salmon swimming upstream. This place was packed. Milkshakes might have brought the boys to the yard, but thirty-five-year-old action flicks and overpriced snacks brought millennials back to the movie theater. It had worked for me, at least.

That was something unique to our generation, the thirty and fortysomething "kids" caught between digital and analog—we longed for experience. Memories, not stuff.

Which was why along with tonight's screening of the so-called holiday classic, local artisans had gathered throughout the lobby to hock their wares and treats, everything from hand poured candles—some of which were shaped and painted like candy cane dicks—to boozy cake pops. I was more than ready to knock back a few of those.

Cake pops, I meant. Not dicks. There was only one dick on my mind these days.

As we waited in line for the photo booth, I couldn't help but think about a certain photographer who lived next door. More specifically, about the showstopping kiss he had planted on me earlier in the week.

The first kiss to end all first kisses.

And it had happened under the mistletoe, of all places. In front of my sister and our friends. No wonder Austin had turned tail and bolted for his door the second after it had ended. He wasn't the only one who had been embarrassed.

I had thought about kissing my sexy Santa for months now, but in all of my dreams and fantasies—and there were a lot to choose from—none had included an audience. Well, maybe one, but that was a very, *very* different kind of fantasy, one that had come on the tail end of reading one of Leighton's spicy romances that took place in a sex club.

Our kiss in my apartment wasn't exactly what I had envisioned, and yet, I wouldn't take it back for all the presents in Santa's . . . sack. That was another new development—I had somewhat of a Santa kink. Though, was it really a kink if I only wanted to fuck one particular Santa?

Inquiring minds need to know.

The sudden waft of some nutty, sweet concoction had me spinning in my heels. Well, *heel*, since I was still rocking the Aircast. "Something smells incredible," Riley said.

Bowie pointed to a small cart just beyond the photo booth. "Chestnuts."

"Roasted on an open fire, I presume?"

He shrugged. "In West Hollywood? Doubtful. More like toasted in a microwave oven."

Nora and I both giggled at his Jonathan Bailey-esque pronunciation of *mick-ro-wave*. For someone who had never been to the U.K., I had somehow surrounded myself with British transplants. Then again, that wasn't difficult to do in Los Angeles. There was a Tom Holland hopeful lurking in every Coffee Bean & Tea Leaf.

"Where are Leighton and Killian tonight?" Riley asked.

"Oh, she's hard at work preparing for that *Snow Place Like L.A.* thing. There was a beret emergency."

"The worst kind of emergency, if you ask me." Devin rested their hands on Riley's pregnant belly. After a grueling in vitro process, the couple were expecting their first baby this spring. "Babe, whatever happened to that beret I got on our honeymoon?"

While the two of them regaled us with some adorable story about matching raspberry berets that would make Prince proud, my thoughts wandered to my sister.

I really should call her.

Leighton had been tinsel deep in final fittings and whatever else it took to put together a capsule collection as of late. Between that and my sudden influx of needy clients, we hadn't exchanged so much as a text message in days—not since the photo shoot and subsequent decorating party at my place.

Nonetheless, Leighton would have her own cheering section at her upcoming runway show if I had it my way, and let's face it, I usually did. I knew she was nervous—hell, I was nervous for her—but that was to be expected. The best things in life were usually the scariest, too.

Big jobs, big adventures, big love. I should know. They all terrified the shit out of me.

"Nellie, you coming?"

"Hm?" My cheeks warmed when I found four sets of eyes staring back at me. How long had I tuned them out for?

"It's our turn to take a picture," Riley said, smiling.

"Oh, you guys can do one without me."

"What?" Nora protested. "You have to be in it."

"Seriously, it's fine. I don't want to get in the way of your . . . cute couples' shit."

She rolled her eyes. "Please. I live with a British gentleman who paints my nails while feeding me scones *he* baked. I've had my fill of cute couple shit."

Bowie's hand coasted lower over her back. "Funny, I didn't hear you complaining this morning when I filled you with my—"

"Wow, look at all the snow." Nora jumped forward, evading his hand—and the end of that sentence. "It's like we're in . . . Utah or something."

Before we so much as set foot inside the giant plastic orb, a familiar voice rasped, "Of all the gin joints."

My lips parted on a gasp. It wasn't enough that we lived next door to each other or that he had knocked me flat on Thanksgiving. I could even come up with some veiled excuse for bumping into him at the pet store photo shoot, but come on now—this was getting ridiculous.

Maybe I really had stumbled into *It's a Wonderful Life* after all, because it seemed like Clarence, my guardian angel, had intervened yet again. That or Austin was the only photographer in the greater Los Angeles area.

I twisted to find him leaning against his tripod, scratching his beard. It had only been a few days since I'd seen him, yet his beard looked bushier than ever.

All the better to scrape my thighs with.

Reindeer and snowflakes adorned his red knit sweater. The sleeves had been pushed up to his elbows, exposing the black-and-gray swirls of ink beneath. *Oh, baby.* What I wouldn't give to see those tattooed mitts wrapped around my throat. No wonder he wore fur-lined gloves when he was dressed as his alter ego.

Maybe if I was a good girl, Father Christmas would let me call him daddy.

"I think that's a different movie," I told him when I finally found my voice.

Those dark chocolate eyes of his sparkled with interest.

"I didn't take you for a *Die Hard* fan."

"I'm a Christmas fan."

"But *Die Hard* isn't a—"

"Don't say it," I warned, thrusting a finger toward his face. "I will not abide John McClane slander."

He held his hands out in front of him. "I'll keep my slander to myself, then."

"Well, well, well. Look who Santa dragged in."

A familiar figure dressed in black and silver waved from the opposite end of the snow globe. It would have been impossible to miss her and her Tim Burton-esque getup amongst the wintery snowscape.

"Hi, Sloane." I waved. "Good to see you again."

"You, too." She held the flap to the snow globe open as my friends shuffled inside. "Come on, Elle Woods. Into the globe you go."

I quickly scurried over to join the rest in posing for a few photos—one with our arms awkwardly wrapped around each other like high school prom dates, and another where we all tossed up handfuls of the fake snow sprinkled throughout while shouting, "Yippee-ki-yay."

And all the while, Austin's attention never wavered from mine.

After he snapped our photos and Sloane showed us how to download them using the custom QR code, I stepped off to the side. "I'll meet up with you guys later," I told Nora.

"Don't rush," she said around a wink.

Thankfully, the line for the photo booth had died down, probably because the movie was set to start any minute now. Austin removed the camera strap from around his neck and cozied up to my side.

"So . . ."

"So . . ."

"That's some stylish footwear you're rocking." A wide grin spread across his face as he nodded toward my feet.

"Why, thank you."

I knew he wasn't talking about my Marc Jacobs pump. It had taken two spools of silver and gold ribbon, plus a full tube of puffy paint to dress up the Aircast, but I was determined to make the most of my temporary accessory.

"Alright, you two," Sloane interrupted, snatching the camera out of Austin's hand. "Into the bubble you go."

"Oh god, no," he protested. It was too late; Sloane was already shoving us both into the snow globe. "I don't—"

"You don't like having your picture taken, I know. But you owe me one for being here on what should have been my night off, so smile pretty."

He reluctantly sidled up next to me in the pile of faux snow. From the looks of it, his hesitation had less to do with me and more to do with being on the opposite end of the lens.

"Wow, she wasn't kidding. You really don't like being in front of the camera."

"Not at all."

He blew out a breath and wiped his palms awkwardly up and down his side, almost as if he weren't quite sure what to do with them. But that didn't matter. I would be more than happy to show him what to do with his hands.

"Here," I said, threading my fingers through his and wrapping them around my side. He stiffened when I tucked myself against him and rested my other hand over his middle, just above the swell of his belly. "That's better. Now, just pretend you like me for a few seconds."

His eyes darkened. It was like a switch had been flipped. I let out a small squeak when the fingers around my waist tightened, digging into the velvet material draped across my body.

"Oh, Janelle," he crooned, tucking a stray curl behind my ear. His hand skimmed the side of my neck, lower still until he met the collar of my dress. Goose bumps pricked my skin. "We both know there's no need to pretend."

It was a wonder we didn't set the snow globe ablaze.

Even after Sloane took our picture, his fingers stayed laced with mine. "C'mon," he said as he guided me out. "I'll buy you some popcorn."

Be still my beating vagina.

The man knew how to press *all* of my buttons.

Austin

I hadn't been this nervous around a girl since ninth grade, when Penny Moore had invited me over for her "make-out party." The night had ended with me receiving my first ever blow job on her Lisa Frank bedspread, which had lasted for all of seven seconds.

A lot had changed since then, most notably my staying power. However, my lack of dating prowess remained the same.

This isn't even a date, I reminded myself.

Yet here I was, clinging to my gingerbread slushie with one hand while searching for the courage to wrap the other around the woman next to me. Thankfully, she was too focused on her bucket of popcorn—well, her commemorative Nakatomi Tower of popcorn—to notice.

"I'm never going to be able to let this one go," she whispered, turning in her seat to face me. "*Die Hard* is obviously a Christmas movie."

"Are we really having this conversation?"

She bypassed my question, diving into her well-crafted argument. Something told me she'd had this conversation more than once. "First of all, the movie takes place during a Christmas party, on Christmas Eve. On top of that, it's full of popular Christmas songs, memorable one-liners about Santa, and family dysfunction, all of which are classic Christmas tropes."

"Plus, his wife's name is Holly."

She threw her hand up in the air. "I rest my case."

"I knew you were a good lawyer."

"I'm not *that* kind of lawyer. I deal mostly in contract disputes and angry actors."

"But you love it?"

Her pink, plump lips turned up. "Yeah, I do. I appreciate the order and how black and white it is. It's the gray bits that tend to get messy."

"Is that a bad thing?"

She mulled over my question. I resisted the urge to lean forward and press my lips to the wrinkle between her brows. "I used to think so, but I'm starting to see things a little differently."

Because of me. She didn't have to say it; it was written all over her face. And it made me feel fucking amazing.

"What about you?" she asked.

"What about me?"

"How does a man who hates having his photo taken decide to become a photographer?"

I scanned the seats closest to us to make sure we weren't disturbing anybody. Nothing irked me quite like people talking through a movie, except maybe the assholes who didn't properly return their shopping carts. Those people could fuck all the way off by way of a path of Legos.

Fortunately, the few people scattered across the balcony were mostly couples more caught up in each other than the movie on screen.

"It starts with being the only boy in a sea of sisters and ends with dropping out of business school."

She blinked up at me. "I'm not sure which of those is more surprising."

I snagged another handful of popcorn before continuing. "Let's just say my sisters are a lot more gregarious than I am. There was never really an opportunity to be the center of attention, so I sort of just . . . disappeared into the background."

Understanding dawned on her face. "And business school?"

"Just trying to live up to familial expectations, I guess."

"Classic."

"Believe me," I told her around a mouthful of popcorn. "I would have made a shitty analyst."

That was an understatement. Unlike Nellie or my sister, Char, my brain didn't adequately process black and white. There was a reason I photographed in color.

"Well, it all worked out for the best," she said definitively. "You make one hell of a photographer."

"Thank you."

She held my gaze for another second or two before turning back to the movie. There was no missing the way she squirmed in her seat, adjusting the thighs that I longed to feel wrapped around my waist. There was a certain comfort in knowing that she was just as affected as I was.

Feeling suddenly emboldened, I feigned a stretch and wrapped an arm around her seat, resting it on her shoulders.

"Smooth," she said, eyes still focused on the screen.

"I thought so."

Her rumble of laughter vibrated against my side, right where she belonged.

There was no talking after that. Instead, we spent the next hour or so chowing down on popcorn while watching Bruce Willis take down terrorists. By the time we descended the stairs to the balcony hand in hand, Nellie had shifted gears from convincing me that *Die Hard* was a Christmas movie to arguing that Alan Rickman was sexier than Bruce Willis.

"You're absolutely insane," I told her. "In what world is Alan Rickman hotter?"

"You clearly know nothing about the feminine gaze."

We had just cleared the bottom step when she stopped. The color drained from her face, along with the fun, flirty attitude I had come to know so well over the past couple of weeks.

"Nellie, what is it?"

"Tabitha, hello," she said, forcing a smile.

I turned to find a tall blonde woman standing behind me. She was an imposing figure in her mid-forties, maybe, wearing a pristine pantsuit that was far too formal for a night at the movies. Her sleek hairstyle and impeccable posture were the picture-perfect definition of class. She reminded me of my sister, in the worst way possible.

"Janelle," she said curtly. "I'm surprised to see you here."

"Likewise."

"It's my stepson's birthday. *Die Hard* is his favorite movie."

Nellie nodded but said nothing. In the time we had known each other, I had never seen her scared silent, and truth be told, I didn't like it one bit.

Tabitha relinquished the death grip on her designer purse and gestured to me. "Aren't you going to introduce me to your—"

"Neighbor," Nellie finished, quickly releasing my hand from hers. "This is my neighbor, Austin."

Neighbor. Got it.

She might as well have built a picket fence between the two of us then and there. It might have been less painful.

"Nice to meet you."

"You as well," Tabitha said without a hint of emotion. Come to think of it, she bore a startling resemblance to one of the terrorists from the movie. "By the way, Janelle, not to add more to your plate during the weekend, but I have to say, I wasn't really impressed with any of your ideas for the holiday hoopla."

"Oh." Her smile waned. "I'm sorry to hear that."

What the fuck is a holiday hoopla?

This must have been the end of the year office party thing Nellie had mentioned during our first photo session. And from the sounds of things, it wasn't going well.

"If you're not up to planning it, that's fine, but I need to know sooner rather than later. Bennett Studios is still giving us the runaround, and my in-laws are coming to town this week, so the last thing I want to worry about is the godforsaken holiday party." Nellie squirmed under her gaze. "I could always ask Geoffrey—"

"No," Nellie interrupted. "No, I can do it. Just . . . please, give me another chance."

"Of course. We'll talk on Monday." Tabitha tipped her head in lieu of a goodbye, and then she was gone, just as quickly as she had appeared.

"Wow," I said. It was all I could come up with. "So, that was—"

"My boss."

"Got it."

People continued filtering out of the balcony and down the stairs, dodging us and the impromptu roadblock we had created. Nellie didn't seem to notice. She was still frozen to that bottom step, eyes staring blankly across the room. I would have swept her up in my arms and carried her back to that snow globe if I thought she would let me.

But this wasn't one of my nieces' favorite Disney films, and she wasn't a princess waiting to be rescued. That didn't make me want to protect her from the monsters any less.

"How about I take you home? We can even brainstorm ideas for this holiday hoopla thing over some hot chocolate, if you want."

She snapped out of her stupor instantaneously.

"No."

"Apple cider, then?"

"I mean no to all of it."

There was an edge to her tone that I hadn't heard before. Well, maybe once, that day I'd brought over the gift basket and she'd snapped at me.

"This isn't working."

Ouch. It was a phrase I had heard before, more than once, in fact. Though, by my calculations, we were about four months too early for this conversation.

She sighed. "I like you, Austin. You know I do, but I have to focus on work right now. I can't afford any more mistakes."

"Can't we at least enjoy the rest of the evening?"

"You don't get it," she scolded. "You don't have anybody to answer to but yourself. This is everything I've been working for since I was eighteen, and I won't let *this* ruin my plans." My stomach dropped when she gestured between the two of us. "The last thing I need right now is a distraction."

Double ouch.

That wasn't what any guy wanted to hear from the girl he was falling for. Distraction was second only to disappointment.

"Okay, then." The regret on her face would be my undoing. I had to get out of here. Fast. I took a step back. "I'll see you around."

"Wait, Austin. That's not what I meant. You're—"

"A distraction, I know." Her eyes welled with tears. "I won't knock on your door again. Promise."

Chapter Seven

Nellie

I had gotten it wrong yet again.

This wasn't *It's a Wonderful Life* or *Die Hard* or even *Rear Window*. No, I was living in *A Christmas Carol*, and I was the greedy, old bitch who ruined everybody's Christmas.

Minus the ghosts and suffocating nightgown.

"Wow, front-row seats," Nora exclaimed. "I feel like a celebrity."

"You are a celebrity," I reminded her. Just last night, she and Bowie had attended the wrap party for the second season of her show.

She shrugged, tossing her blue hair over one shoulder. "Eh, C-list at best."

That was what I liked about Nora. She had gained so much momentum in her career these last couple of years and still, she acted like a normal person.

Stars, they're just like us.

It was the day of Leighton's knitwear showcase, and the four of us were front row center to the action. We funneled into our chairs beside the runway, Bowie and Killian at our backs. Riley had opted out at the last minute due to morning sickness—in the afternoon—and Devin had stayed home to dote on her. There was no doubt that their bun in the oven would never want for love and attention.

"I'm surprised you didn't bring along your photographer," Nora hedged, arching her brow.

"He's not *my* photographer."

"Oh, that's right. Your Santa," she amended.

"Austin isn't *my* anything," I said, loud enough for the models backstage to hear me. "Not anymore, at least," I added, evening my tone.

Nora blinked back at me, surprised by my outburst, Killian smiled sadly, and Bowie—bless his heart—ducked his head behind his program.

"Do you want to talk about it?" Nora asked.

"No."

She nodded and turned back to the paper program in her hands. "Oh, look. It says—"

"I fucked it up." I tossed my hands in the air.

"I guess we're talking about it," Bowie mumbled.

"I was frustrated—with myself more than anything—and I took it out on Austin, the one person who has been nothing but nice to me. Do you know that he has left a package of my favorite cookies in my mailbox almost every day since my accident? Who does that?"

I'd almost cried the morning after the *Die Hard* fiasco, aka the best non-date I had ever been on, when I'd opened up my mailbox, only to find it empty. It wasn't that I needed more Tim Tams—my pantry was overflowing as it was. I missed the gesture more than anything, the reminder that somebody was thinking about me, looking out for me.

I hadn't realized how much I needed that until it was gone.

"Sounds like a man in love to me," Killian mused.

It couldn't be. Lust, maybe, but not love. Nobody fell in love with somebody over the course of a few weeks. Not outside of the movies or Highlander romance novels, at least.

A distraction.

I buried my face in my hands, recalling the awful things I'd said to him. They had played over and over in my head all week, like a record stuck on repeat. Of course, I had regretted them the second they'd left my mouth, but by then, it had been too late. Sadly, there were no take-backsies when it came to misplaced feelings.

Or STIs, for that matter.

Nora rested her hand on my thigh. "I'm sure it'll all work out. People do and say shitty things in the heat of the moment."

"Besides," Killian said. "Aren't we still doing another round of photos tonight?"

I nodded solemnly. "As far as I know."

Yet another reason to feel sorry for myself. Even after tossing him aside during my moment of weakness, treating him like he was just some random bloke who lived in my building, Austin was still keen on fulfilling his offer.

Stupid jerk.

Why did he have to be so wonderful?

The plan was to meet at Santa Monica Pier, assuming he showed up. I wouldn't blame him if he backed out, not after the things I'd said and, worse, didn't say.

I had racked my mind for a way to apologize to him and come up empty. Words didn't seem like enough, especially since they were what had gotten me into this mess.

I had already decided to throw in the towel on the holiday hoopla, which I was now referring to as the Christmas Crapola. A stupid yacht party or wine tasting wasn't worth throwing away the connection I had with Austin. There were other ways to earn that promotion, and none of them came at the expense of my integrity.

"I hate feeling like this," I whined.

"Like what?"

"A mess." Nora's lips twitched. "I hate mess."

She snorted. "Well, if it makes you feel better, you're a hot mess."

A beautiful mess.

There he was again. In my ear, in my dreams, by the mailbox—there was no getting rid of him. Austin had stamped a place in my heart with that very first box of cookies, and I feared that no amount of milk would ever wash it away.

"Inconvenient is what it is."

Bowie and Killian shared a laugh. "The best things often are," Killian said. "Do you think it was convenient for your sister to pretend to be my fiancée last Christmas?

"Convenient for you, maybe." Though I hadn't known it at the time, Killian had been pining after my sister for nearly a year before their fake engagement. In fact, their farce of a relationship had been my idea. "You're welcome by the way."

He shook his head.

"It definitely wasn't convenient when I fell in love with someone who was supposed to be a casual fling, but turned out to be the love of my life," Nora admitted, resting her hand on Bowie's lap.

I nearly orgasmed on the spot when he wrapped a hand around her neck and tilted her head back to meet his scorching kiss. Damn. I always knew that guy had a kinky side.

It's the quiet ones who bite—or spank—the hardest.

"And I wouldn't change any of it for the world," Bowie said after he removed his tongue from Nora's mouth.

"Nothing at all?" Nora asked, searching his face.

"Nothing. Even the messy, inconvenient bits." He spared a glance in my direction. "It's all part of our story."

I didn't realize I was crying until the first tear hit my wadded-up program. Only this time, it wasn't because I was sad—the pity party was officially canceled—but rather because I was thinking about *my* story. Mine and Austin's, messy bits and all.

Hopefully, it wasn't too late to rewrite our ending.

Austin

When we'd been kids, my sister, Madison, had gone through a phase where she'd only spoken in riddles.

"What kind of cup doesn't hold water? A cupcake."

Stuff like that. The kind of shit that was cute when a nine-year-old said it, but insufferable coming from an adult. Eventually, she'd outgrown the habit, though I knew for a fact that she had a special place in her heart for word puzzles to this very day.

I would have to run this one by her during our next phone call.

What's a single thirty-four-year old's favorite ride at Santa Monica Pier? The emotional roller coaster.

And the crowd goes mild.

"Careful of the ice cream, Leighton."

"I can't help it," she cried. "It's dripping all over me."

We were finishing up the last of today's shooting schedule. We had already snapped four pictures before the sun had gone down. The only one left to go was their photo in front of the Ferris wheel.

In the original photo, a four- or five-year-old Leighton swung her legs off a bench while enjoying an ice cream cone as big as her face. Beside her, Nellie, who couldn't have been more than one or two at the time, clung to a cheap stuffed animal—clearly a prize won at one of the nearby game stalls. A glowing Ferris wheel backlit the two of them, just as it did now.

"Alright, we got it."

"Oh, thank god." Leighton tossed what was left of her ice cream into the nearby trash can. "I need to wash this off. It's too cold for ice cream."

She wasn't kidding. Fifty degrees was downright freezing by Los Angeles's standards, and yet, it hadn't deterred locals and tourists alike from visiting the pier tonight. The place was bustling with folks of all ages, many of whom had come to see tonight's holiday-themed lighting display. They lit the Ferris wheel up year-round, but only in December could you see a ninety-foot-tall, super-sized snowman, animated to wave merrily over the Pacific Ocean.

"Can we talk?"

I sucked in a breath and twisted to face the woman I had been avoiding for days. *Old habits die hard.* We hadn't so much as texted until today, when I'd reached out to confirm the time of our photo shoot.

I'd wanted to call her. I had even written out a script, which, spoiler alert, was about as good as my riddle. As per usual, my insecurities had gotten the best of me, and the incessant questions had taken the leftovers. *If she wanted to talk to me, she could just knock on my door, couldn't she? Does she really just consider me a distraction? Will I ever be enough for her?*

That last one hurt the most, probably because it wasn't the first time it had crossed my mind. On the contrary, it was an obstacle I had been working to overcome with my therapist for a while now—blame it on thirty-plus years of being the family outcast.

That was my issue to work through, not hers, but I still needed to know if there was even the slightest chance that we might have a shot.

"Sure."

Her eyes skated over the pier. "Here?"

"Unless you want to do it up there?" Her mouth dropped open when I pointed toward the Ferris wheel. As a photographer, I was very well versed in both human emotions and facial expressions. I knew fear when I saw it. "I was just kidding. What did you want—"

"Okay."

"Okay, what?"

She nodded toward the wheel. "Let's go."

"You're serious."

"About us, yes."

There was still an us. If that were the case, I would climb the fucking Ferris wheel.

"Let's go."

Leighton stopped us on her way back from the restroom. "Killian's picking us up in five minutes. Wait, where are you guys going?"

"To ride the Ferris wheel," I told her.

She scrunched her eyebrows together, confused. "*You're* riding the Ferris wheel?" The question was directed solely at Nellie.

"That's right."

"But—"

"Oh, look, there's no line. I'll call you tomorrow, sis." She caught my hand in hers and dragged me toward the entrance to the ride, pausing only to call out, "Great show today!"

I waved goodbye to a dumbstruck Leighton.

Two minutes later, we were seated in a private car, a partially enclosed orb with a bench on either side and an attached umbrella overhead to block out the California sunshine. Not that that would be an issue at night.

Nellie took the seat across from me . . . at least until the ride started. The second we shoved off from the ground, she leapt across the space, planting herself beside me.

For a minute, we just took in the view, or at least I did. She kept her eyes firmly shut and her hands clenched tight. I was starting to think this might have been a bad idea. From the looks of it, she was about three seconds away from hyperventilating.

"Nellie, we can ask them to stop the—"

"I owe you a huge apology," she blurted out.

"What?"

She smiled sadly. "I never should have snapped at you at the theater. I was frustrated by the whole holiday party crap and, frankly, a little embarrassed—"

"You had nothing to be embarrassed about."

"Believe me, I know." She fumbled with her scarf. "I just . . . It was a vulnerable moment for me, and let's just say, I'm not very good at feeling vulnerable in front of other people."

That made two of us.

"That's not an excuse for treating you like crap or pretending like you were just some random guy, when you're anything but."

"It's okay. I understand."

She arched her brow. "But?"

My lips kicked up to one side. "But, I also don't want to get in the way of anything."

"You're not," she said, shaking her head with vigor. "*Holy fuck, we're up high.*"

I wrapped an arm around her shoulders and closed the distance between us. With my other hand, I gripped her chin, turning her face back toward mine.

"Eyes on me," I growled. She must have recognized the warning in my tone because her eyes snapped up to meet mine. "Were you going to tell me you were afraid of heights?"

"No."

Well, at least she was honest.

"Why did you say yes to riding the Ferris Wheel?"

When her attention started to wander, I lowered my hand to her throat. There was no real pressure, just enough to make her squirm, no doubt soaking the seat beneath us. She could tell me to stop at any time and I would. But we both knew she wanted this.

We both knew she was my naughty girl. And naughty girls needed to be punished.

"I don't do well at giving up control."

"That's now what I asked." She practically purred when the hand around her throat slightly tightened. "Why did you say yes to riding the Ferris Wheel, Janelle?"

Her eyes narrowed. "Because you asked me to."

That was all I needed to know. I slammed my lips down on hers, tangling our tongues together when she opened her mouth on a gasp. There was nothing sweet about this kiss. This was a good old-fash-ioned, desperate tongue fucking, a duel to the finish, only there were no losers here.

She threaded her fingers through my hair, scraping my scalp in a way that sent shivers down my spine, all the way to my cock. This time, I was the one moaning. "Fuck, Janelle." I groaned into her mouth.

Before either of us had time to overthink it, I released her throat and lowered my hand to the hem of her skirt. Inch by inch, my fingers danced across her upper thigh, until finally nudging the wet material covering her core.

She tore her lips away. "What are you doing?"

"Making you feel good."

Her pupils flared with intrigue. "People might see."

"Let me worry about that."

Truth be told, there was nothing to worry about. It was dark out, save for the glowing snowman on the side of the wheel, the compartment beside us was empty, and nobody would be able to see what I was about to do to her thanks to the wall surrounding our seats.

"Do you trust me?" She nodded. "Do you want me to make you come?" Another nod. "Then widen your legs, sit back, and enjoy the ride."

I know I will.

She did as I asked, allowing me plenty of room to access her pussy. I dipped under the lace band, scraping through the thin path of pubic hair paving the way to her clit.

Her head lolled back against my arm when I circled the bud.

"*Fuck*," she groaned. "Please don't stop."

That's right, baby. Beg.

I slid my fingers lower, dragging them through the wetness at her entrance. She was melting faster than the ice cream cone, dripping all over my hand. I needed a taste.

I swirled my fingers through her juices once more before removing them completely. She whined, then moaned when I licked them clean.

No use crying over spilt pussy juices, baby.

"Been dying to taste you for months now."

She blushed. "And?"

"And now I want more."

There would be plenty of time for that later. I planned to spend tonight, tomorrow, and hopefully the rest of our lives with my tongue buried between her thighs. That required a little more space and a lot more time, both of which we didn't currently have.

My fingers delved back inside her panties.

Her warm breath fanned the bare spot beneath my beard, while my thumb toyed with her clit. Teasing, tormenting. *Exquisite torture.*

"Please, Austin," she begged. I nearly came in my pants when she nipped my neck, no doubt leaving her mark. *Cheeky brat.*

"Only good girls get what they want for Christmas." I slid my middle finger inside until I was knuckle deep. She was tight, but she was also dripping wet. "Have you been a good girl, Janelle?"

She shook her head, muttering a barely intelligible "no" against my neck.

I doubled my efforts, adding a second finger. To the casual onlooker, Nellie and I might look like a couple enjoying a romantic ride on the Ferris wheel. Little did they know that I was drawing figure eights inside her cunt.

I crowded in, pinning her back against the wall while my fingers plunged in and out of her. Faster, deeper. I knew we had to be making a mess, what with the wet, squelching noises we were making, and yet I couldn't be bothered to care. Nellie was hardly the first girl to get fingerbanged on the Ferris wheel, and she certainly wouldn't be the last.

My free hand threaded through her hair, tugging her head back until her eyes met mine.

"Are you a naughty girl?"

"Yes," she answered with zero hesitation.

"Are you *my* naughty girl?"

She fisted my jacket when my fingers scissored inside her, brushing against that spot that I knew would set her off any second now. Her pussy pulsed in response.

"*Yesss.*"

"Good *fucking* answer, baby."

I thrust my fingers inside her again and again, all the while rolling my thumb over her clit. And to her credit, Nellie's gaze never wavered from mine. Not until I leaned forward and nipped her bottom lip. It was that last little bite of pain—pun intended—that sent her flying over the edge.

Only this time, there was no fear or trepidation. This time, she had somebody to catch her.

Chapter Eight

December 18th

Nellie

I was going to fuck Santa Claus.

Correction: He was going to fuck me—hard—and then frost me like a cookie.

Not that you would hear me complaining; he wasn't the only one who had been dying for a taste.

My panties were clean soaked through by the time we stumbled into Austin's apartment, a few minutes after midnight. From there, he was on me. A frenzy of hands, lips, and teeth.

He had already stroked me through the most intense orgasm of my life on the Santa Monica Pier, effectively helping me overcome two of my greatest fears in one fell swoop—heights and sex in public.

It wasn't enough, though. It would never be enough, not until I made him mine, once and for all.

Austin had stoked a fire inside my veins that any second now, would singe us both to a crisp.

What a way to go.

His nose skated a line down the center of my thong, nuzzling deeper when he reached the damp fabric clinging to my crease like a second skin. I had lost my skirt before the door had snicked shut behind us. Tights and shoes, too, which meant I was bare from the waist down, save for the scrap of lace barely containing my pussy.

I tried not to feel too self-conscious when he inhaled my scent. Vagina smelled like vagina, no matter how much you tried to dress it up.

Austin didn't seem to mind. On the contrary, my knees buckled when he let out a warm breath, tickling every follicle of hair decorating my pussy. Thankfully, he was there to catch me. Again.

"Stand still, baby," he whispered against my panties, teasing my lips through the soft material. "Let me play with this pussy."

A surge of confidence rocketed through me. "It would be a lot easier if I were naked."

"Somebody's impatient."

His cocky laughter vibrated against my clit. *Fucking hell.* Forget vibrators, somebody could make a killing auctioning off bearded men with belly laughs. At this rate, I might come again before he even got my panties off.

I thrust my hips forward, my patience running thin.

"It's cute that you think you're calling the shots." His hands roved up the back of my thighs, coasting over the curve of my ass until they reached the scalloped edge of my panties. "But we both know who's in charge here."

He tangled his fingers through the straps on either side of my hips. "Isn't that right, naughty girl?"

"Yes, *Daddy.*"

His fingers froze. I tilted my chin down to meet his fiery gaze.

"Say it again," he growled.

My nipples swelled at the commanding tone in his voice. Gone was the cat dad who lived next door, the quiet neighbor who had brought me "get well soon" cookies. This was the man who had threatened to put me on the naughty list when I sat on his lap, the kinky fucker who less than an hour ago, had made me squirt all over a theme park ride.

Sweet, neighborly Austin was gone; bad Santa had come to play.

I threaded my fingers through his hair and pressed his face further into my pussy, gasping when his nose collided with my clit. "Please, Daddy. Make me come."

Time stood still for exactly two seconds, or maybe thirty—there was no way to know for sure. Not in the depths of his dark living room, illuminated only by the soft white glow of tree lights. Neither of us had had the will to make it to his bedroom, let alone the couch.

And then, in the blink of an eye, the lips pressed against my mound crooked up in a mischievous grin. At the same time, the fingers knotted through my thong yanked, snapping it off my body.

There was no suppressing my cry when in the next second, he thrust his tongue deep.

"*Fuck,*" I half-whispered, half-groaned. I didn't even recognize the sound of my own voice.

The rough edges of his beard scratched at my thighs and labia while his tongue tore through layer after layer of my pussy, eventually drawing a line up to my clit. When he circled the small bud and sucked, my legs instinctively tried to trap his head in place.

There was something so empowering about seeing him like this, on his knees, holding me up with his massive fingers, eyes full of hunger and reverence. This man could snap me in half if he wanted to. Yet here he was, licking me, savoring me like I was his last meal on Earth.

I sucked in a breath when he added first one finger, and then another to the mix, crooking them inside me like he was beckoning me closer. How much closer could I possibly get? The man already had his lips, tongue, and fingers buried in my cunt.

"Austin, I need you."

"You've got me, baby."

He managed to add a third finger. "No." I gasped. "I need more. I need you inside me."

His eyes flashed. Before I knew it, we were moving again, only this time he was gently lowering me to the living room rug. "Is this okay?" he asked before shoving my sweater over my head and undoing my bra.

"Uh-huh."

"You deserve to be taken in a bed and worshiped for hours."

I don't know about that. I felt pretty fucking worshiped already.

A soft smile tugged at my lips. "I'm not going to break if you fuck me on the floor, Austin."

He let out a shuddering breath before leaning forward to rest his forehead against mine. "That mouth."

"This mouth?" I closed the gap between us, nipping at his lips.

His hand snaked down and around my neck, applying the lightest pressure to my throat, just enough to send a dark thrill shooting through my veins like lightning. He smirked, no doubt loving the way my pulse beat wildly against his hold.

"You're asking for trouble."

His voice was soft, almost teasing. But the edge to it made me shiver.

I licked my lips, my mouth suddenly bone-dry. "That's what naughty girls do."

One corner of his mouth hooked up in a wicked, wolfish grin.

I sat back, enjoying the view while he undressed, adding his discarded clothing to the growing pile on the floor. My fantasies hadn't done him justice. In reality, he was bigger, thicker, hairier—a beast in human form.

Santa baby.

Thin black curls peppered across his chest and bulging belly, like an arrow pointing straight toward his girthy cock. The reindeer tattoo inked just above his right thigh made me giggle. The demanding look on his face did not.

"Turn over, baby," he ordered while rolling on a condom. I opened my mouth to argue, but quickly closed it when the sharp crack of his hand hitting my thigh echoed through the room. "Now."

"*Yesss,*" I squealed.

"Yes, what?"

"Yes, Daddy."

He rubbed a hand over the spot he had slapped. "Good girl."

I rolled to my stomach, careful not to knock into the tree, and pulled my knees up so my ass was in the air, on full display. The loud moan he emitted let me know he appreciated my efforts.

"I fucking love this ass." He smoothed a hand over first one cheek, and then the other. "You don't know how many times I've jerked off thinking about touching you here, licking you here." I jerked when a finger probed the tight ring of muscle between my cheeks. "Fucking you here."

I moaned into my shoulder.

"Would you like that, baby girl?" he rasped. "Me inside your ass."

"I— I don't know."

It wasn't something I had ever given much consideration to, a taboo subject amongst my friends back home. And yet, the thought of

Austin taking me there, tunneling his dick in and out of that forbidden hole, didn't scare me. On the contrary, it felt dirty and amazing.

Naughty.

"Maybe."

"We can revisit that another time." He moved into position behind me, nudging me legs wider to carve out space for his thick thighs and thicker cock. The blunt tip of his crown pressed against my entrance. "For now, I'm going to fuck this pussy."

"*Oh, god,*" I cried when he pushed inside of me, bottoming out in one thrust.

I was stretched so tight, the sense of fullness nearly overwhelmed me. It felt so good. So freaking perfect. Like my body had been made for him and him alone.

"Fuck, Janelle. You're so goddamn tight." He rolled his hips forward and back before pulling out of me completely, only to shove himself back in. "This first time is going to be fast, baby," he muttered, gasping for air.

At least I wasn't the only one struggling to breathe.

It took me a minute to match his pace, but after that, it was a race to the finish. I squeezed my eyes shut as he pistoned in and out of me, his balls slapping my pussy with each thrust. The onslaught of sensations was nearly overwhelming—the smack of our bodies, the sweat beading between. My toes curled while my fingers dug into the rug beneath us, desperately searching for an anchor to cling to.

"*Austin.*"

It wasn't so much a word as it was a needy whimper, a desire to be filled, used, tossed around like a rag doll.

"I've got you, baby."

An arm snaked around my middle, pulling me up until my back met his front. I gasped as he continued his relentless rhythm, pumping inside me at a new angle that let him go deeper than before. My head lolled back against his chest on a groan. One hand tweaked my nipples while the other rubbed firm, tight circles over the swollen nub of my clit.

"Let go, Janelle," he growled into my neck. "Give it all to Daddy."

The orgasm barreled into me like a runaway train, ruining me. My hips jerked erratically, thighs slapping against his. Bright lights burst behind my eyelids as my pussy convulsed around him, milking his cock while he groaned out my name.

When we both eventually caught our breaths, Austin dropped us onto our sides without removing his cock.

"Ho-ho-holy shit," he panted, sounding like he'd run a marathon. Before Austin, I would have said that there was no bigger high than finishing a marathon. Now, I wasn't so sure.

I laughed and then moaned when another shudder rippled through my still very full pussy.

"You okay?"

My head bobbed against his arm.

"Did I break you?"

This time, I shook it.

"Can you speak?"

"In a minute."

He smoothed a hand up and down my side while I caught my breath . . . and regained speech function. A sudden thought rushed over me.

"Let's take a picture."

He lifted his head. "Now?"

"Yes." I turned my head and found his lips, coaxing them open with a slow, wet kiss. "I don't ever want to forget this moment or how incredible I feel."

He nodded and kissed me again.

I barely moved when he went to fetch his camera—and remove the condom. Instead, I lay back on his floor, stretching my well-used muscles while counting the lights on the Christmas tree.

A soft purr from my right had me twisting my head.

"You must be Ralphie." *The mysterious third cat.* His tail flopped over the edge of the couch. "I apologize for defiling your dad like that."

"Are you talking to yourself?"

Austin lowered himself back beside me, this time with his camera in hand.

"Your cat," I said, pointing toward the black blob on the couch. "He's a little bit of a pervert."

"Like father, like son."

I laughed. When he sat up, intent on capturing my smile, I held up a hand. "No, both of us."

"What?"

The uncertainty in his voice cracked something in my chest. From what he had told me about his family, it sounded like Austin wasn't used to being the center of attention. But everybody deserved to feel special, especially soft, squishy daddy doms who dressed up as Santa Claus.

I stole the camera from his hands before he had a chance to argue. "Smile, Austin."

It wasn't until much later, in between bouts of lovemaking and grilled cheese sandwiches, that I snuck a peek at the photo, only to find that Austin had indeed smiled. *I guess he takes orders as well as he gives them.* But it wasn't the sappy grin on his face that took me by surprise, so much as the direction of his gaze.

He wasn't looking at the camera; he was looking at me.

Austin

I woke up to a smile on my face and slender fingers wrapped around my cock.

Best. Christmas. Ever.

A weight had been lifted off my chest last night, which left plenty of room for the woman draped across my body.

Right where she belonged.

"Morning," I mumbled, my voice thick with sleep.

Nellie tilted her head back to meet my gaze. Frizzy, blonde waves framed her face, the aftermath of going to sleep without drying her hair. "Good morning." The contrast of her sweet, innocent tone and wicked grin made my cock jerk.

Just as I had suspected, Nellie was a sexual dynamo. Her hunger matched my own.

"Looks like you've got your hands full." I nodded my head toward the erection tenting the sheet.

"It's fun to play with." Her fingers rolled over the head, slicking the precum leaking from my tip down my shaft. "Seriously, how do you not play with it all day, every day?"

She didn't give me a chance to answer.

"And *this* is my favorite part—the head. It's pink and cute."

Pink and cute? She made my cock sound like Hello Kitty.

I couldn't find the will to protest. Fuck, I could barely breath when she was working my dick like a goddamn stripper pole.

"Although, I'm also partial to these." She scraped a nail down my length, tracing the bulging pink lines. "The veins."

A shiver racked my body.

"They look painful."

"Are you planning on doing something to fix that?" I growled.

"Maybe."

A groan rumbled out of my chest when her grip tightened, pumping me once, twice, three times. Hand jobs were underrated. Every guy enjoyed getting his dick sucked, but a slow, lazy hand job went a long way.

Somebody ought to put that on a mug.

I'm easy like a Sunday morning . . . hand job.

My cock protested when she stilled her movement. "Then again, I really should check my email."

I shot up before she had a chance to escape, rolling her beneath me and caging her in against the mattress. The tits that I was now very well acquainted with bounced beneath her shirt. She was still gloriously naked from the waist down, which made it easy to wedge two fingers inside her to test her readiness. My other hand gripped her chin, holding her in place while I plundered her mouth.

"Austin." She moaned breathlessly. "I want you inside me."

"You gonna let me take you bare, baby?"

We'd had the customary birth control discussion in the wee hours of the morning. I knew she had an I.U.D., but there was a lot more to safe sex than preventing pregnancy. Neither of us had been with anybody else for months, and we had both been tested since then, so she knew exactly what I was asking for.

Her trust.

"Yes."

"You want Daddy to fill you up with this cock?"

She groaned out her assent when I removed my fingers and replaced them with my cock, rocking forward into her weeping cunt. *Fuck.* I dropped my head into the crook of her shoulder, peppering her neck with kisses while I tried to catch my breath.

She felt good.

So. Fucking. Good.

I would be lucky if I lasted a minute, less if she kept squeezing me like that. I groaned again and lifted my head. Her smile was a dead giveaway. She knew exactly what she was doing to me.

"Why do you have to do that?"

She batted her lashes. "Do what?"

"Be a naughty girl."

"You love it."

I love y—

I barely resisted the urge to say it—the phrase that until now, had always been reserved for friends and family. Instead, I powered into her, swallowing up her cries with my lips. It was the only surefire way to keep myself from saying something stupid and scaring her off. Best to keep my mouth occupied, kissing, licking, nibbling.

"I've got you, baby," I chanted, pinning her hips to the mattress as I increased my tempo. Nellie's hand slipped between our bodies, circling her clit. "There's my naughty girl. Touch yourself, baby. Come all over Daddy's cock."

Daddy loves you.

Fuck, there they were again. Those three little words that were anything but. With the exception of the woman beneath me, I had never been much for little things. I had the beard and belly to prove it. And yet, in this moment, I knew there was nothing I wouldn't do to protect Janelle Wheatley. To guard her heart, mind, body, and soul.

All mine.

"More," she cried, meeting my punishing thrusts.

I circled her throat with my hand and whispered against her lips, "*Everything.*"

That was a promise.

"This is the most ridiculous kitchen gadget I've ever seen in my life." She squealed when I handed her a plate with the finished breakfast sandwich. "And I absolutely love it."

She pecked my lips before tearing into the sandwich. I smirked, knowing that I was the reason she had worked up an appetite.

It had been going on noon by the time we'd made it out of bed. Nellie, clad only in my favorite Goo Goo Dolls tee and her Aircast, had perched herself on my countertop, insistent on a front-row seat to my breakfast making. Not that there was much to it. My breakfast sandwich maker, a takeaway from last year's gift exchange game with my family, did most of the work for me.

"Okay, why does this taste so good?"

"I told you."

"Seriously," she said around another bite of sandwich. "I'm never going to be able to look at a breakfast sandwich the same way again."

Egg yolk dripped down the corner of her mouth. She eyed me through a hooded gaze when I leaned forward and captured her lips—yellow goo and all—with mine.

"Mmm," I said, licking my lips. "You taste good."

"I doubt that. I haven't even brushed my teeth yet."

"Janelle, I had my tongue in your asshole last night. Do you really think a little morning breath will bother me?"

Her hand shot out to cover my mouth, just as somebody knocked at the door. There was a very short list of people who would show up at my door unannounced, so chances were good it was either Sloane, the UPS. delivery guy, or the Girl Scout who lived in 4B.

Unfortunately, there was no package or box of cookies waiting on my porch when I opened the door, but rather my assistant.

"You're not dressed yet?" she asked before storming into my apartment.

"Hello to you, too."

"We have the Christmas train at two, and it's going to take at least an hour to get there. I told you I would pick you up at—"

She stopped when she noticed the woman sitting on my counter. The one not wearing pants.

"Well, well, well. I must have missed the breakfast invitation."

Nellie bit her lip. "Hi, Sloane."

"Hello, again. I'll get back to you in a second." She spun in her sky-high heels to face me. "*You* forgot."

It wasn't a question.

"I was a little . . . tied up."

Nellie's cheeks flushed, no doubt remembering the way I had bound her wrists to my bed frame last night for our second round of lovemaking. For nearly an hour, she had pushed and pulled at the restraints, desperate to thrust herself against the lips and fingers tormenting her pussy.

And she'd loved every second of it. We both had.

Nellie's moans had turned to cries, then eventually screams. Loud enough to wake up the entire apartment complex. *Poor Mrs. Lyons.* She'd nearly shot off the mattress when I'd finally let her come, first on my fingers, and then again on my cock with her good leg draped over my shoulder. We'd both been drenched with sweat and . . . other stuff by the time I'd lifted her into my arms and carried us both to the shower.

There, I held her under the spray until the water had run cold. Touching her, loving her, memorizing every freckle and scar because they were equally beautiful. And she'd done the same, tracing over my tattoos with her fingers and lips before dropping to her knees and taking me into her mouth.

I might have blacked out when my cock had nudged the back of her throat. Who would have thought that the bubblegum princess who lived next door would be a world-class cocksucker?

My naughty girl.

By the time we'd piled back into my bed—after a much needed sheet change, of course—it had nearly been four a.m. Which was why we were only getting around to eating breakfast now. I had even convinced her to take the morning off. It wasn't an entire day, but it was a start.

I would take whatever she was willing to give me and happily beg for more. Because when it came to Nellie, I wanted it all.

"Give me ten minutes," I told Sloane.

I set my coffee aside and took off for my bedroom, pausing when I reached the edge of the couch. Nellie's brows shot up when I turned back around and pulled her into my body for a quick, searing kiss.

"So, it's like that then?" Sloane interjected.

Nellie giggled against my lips. A slight shove to my chest had me pulling away. "Go," she said.

I raced for the bedroom. It only took me three minutes to change, plus another three to wash my face, brush my teeth, and run a quick comb through my beard. I might have spent an extra minute moisturizing my beard, too, which was thicker than usual. Nellie hadn't seemed to mind last night, but the beard burn on her inner thighs told a different story this morning.

I had just finished loading up my camera gear when voices filtered around the corner and into the living room.

"Things seem to be going well for you two."

"You could say that," Nellie said.

"I hope you know how much he means to me, how incredible he is." Sloane's words warmed my heart. Through all the ups and downs of the last few years, she had always been my one-woman hype team. "Seriously, you will never find a better person than Austin. He just . . . takes a while to warm up sometimes."

Nellie's giggle echoed through the apartment. "I'm starting to get that."

"Just, please don't hurt my boy."

There was a short pause before Nellie's reply. "He might be your boy, Sloane, but he's my man."

Fuck. Was it too late to cancel today's photoshoot?

"I am?" I asked.

Nellie gasped when I rounded the corner, dropping her plate—and what was left of her sandwich—to the floor. It crashed against the tiles, fracturing into several pieces.

"Shit!" Nellie shouted.

"Just stay there a minute." I set my camera bag aside and quickly slipped into my shoes. "Dustpan, hall closet," I told Sloane.

"I'm on it."

While she raced to get it, I made a beeline for the kitchen. More specifically, for the woman on the verge of tears, clawing at the hem of her shirt. Well, my shirt.

"I'm so sorry, Austin," she said, lips trembling. "I can't believe I did—*oof.*"

I scooped her up without a word and carried her out of there, depositing her back on her feet once we reached the safety of the living room.

"Don't worry about it," I told her, attempting to ease her worries. "It's just a plate, and not even one of my favorites." She didn't look so sure, so I combed my fingers through her hair and added, "Actually, I've got a couple of ugly mugs my sister's kids made me if you feel like you need to break more shit."

Her shoulders shook with laughter. And then, almost as if a lightbulb went off, her eyes shot to mine, widening with glee.

"The Christmas Crapola."

"The what?"

She was already halfway to the bedroom, mumbling something about a "beautiful mess" along the way. Not a minute later, she was back, only this time her arms were overflowing with last night's clothes. "I've got some calls to make," she said, hurriedly racing for the door. "Oh, and Austin?"

"Yeah?"

"You are."

My brows furrowed. "I am what?"

"My man."

Damn straight I was.

Chapter Nine

December 21st

Nellie

I'd spent the summer before college in Australia, learning to surf on Bondi Beach. The following winter, I'd taken a stab at ice climbing during an internship in Calgary . . . and promptly discovered that I was *not* a fan of ice anything. I had visited nineteen nations, eaten international cuisine from around the globe, and even ridden a camel or two, all before I'd turned twenty-six.

I thought I had seen it all.

That was, until I saw my boss beating the crap out of a Fisher-Price dollhouse with a baseball bat.

"Take that, Debra," Tabitha cried, bringing the bat down once more. "My." *Thwack.* "Stuffing." *Thwack.* "Isn't." *Thwack.* "Dry." *Thwack.*

The dollhouse splintered in half, sending plastic toy furniture shooting off in every direction. I could practically hear the collective gasps of millennial girls everywhere.

"Now I understand the jumpsuits and goggles," Holly, the office manager, mumbled. I had never seen Holly outside the confines of her desk, let alone dressed in a candy-cane-striped jumpsuit, wielding an ax. "Thank you for this, Janelle."

"My pleasure."

Shattering that plate at Austin's place the other day had been the best thing that could have possibly happened to me. Strike that. Getting railed by Austin the night prior had been, followed shortly by a clean bill of health at the doctor's office yesterday, which meant no more walking boot for me. But that broken plate had been a close third.

For weeks, I had been racking my brain to come up with an idea for the holiday hoopla, something elegant and luxurious, perfect, even. Something that I thought would match the partners' lifestyles.

And then, it'd hit me. Maybe their lives weren't perfect, after all.

Maybe, like the rest of us, they also had student debt to worry about and families that drove them up the wall. Maybe for them, the holidays weren't so much a time to reflect on what had already happened as they were a reminder of things yet to come—deadlines, contracts, tax season.

Maybe they were frustrated—with their partners, their siblings, themselves. It was only natural. Those feelings didn't just disappear when you turned forty or found "the one" or got the promotion you desperately wanted.

It was a bitter pill to swallow, but thankfully, it went down well with a sledgehammer. Because nothing said Christmas quite like a roomful of lawyers going apeshit on the ghosts of appliances past.

Whoever had come up with the concept of a rage room deserved the Bennett Studios account more than I did. *Rudolph's Rage Room* was something extra special. In addition to the typical office furniture, outdated appliances, and dishware, Rudolph's also offered a holi-day-specific room featuring Christmas trees, wrapped presents, and plastic reindeer, all of which were fair game for destruction.

Yippee-ki-yay, motherfucker.

Just ten minutes ago, the entire staff had watched in equal parts awe and horror as Mr. Faison had smashed a landline phone to smithereens using nothing but an oversized lollipop.

Talk about a beautiful mess.

"It seems like everybody is having a good time."

Holly smiled. "Are you kidding? I'm coming back next week with my friend, Jill. She just caught her husband slipping his package un-derneath her sister's tree."

I wonder what kind of juicy gossip Holly has on the rest of us.

"Janelle."

My spine straightened at the sound of Tabitha's voice. She had traded in her weapon and goggles for a bottle of water. Her normally well-coiffed bob was slightly askew. It was refreshing to see her like this, to know that she wasn't the emotionless machine she often portrayed herself to be.

"I have to say, I was surprised when you came up with the idea of a rage room."

"But?" I asked, hedging my bets.

Her lips twitched. "But, it's absolutely perfect. I can't speak for anybody else, but the holidays always stress me out."

I lowered my voice. "Debra?"

She inched closer. "My mother-in-law."

We shared a small laugh, the sound lost amongst a sea of crashes and bangs.

"By the way, assuming the Bennett Studios contract goes through, I want you to take the lead."

I blinked. "Really?"

"Of course. You're the best junior associate we have. You didn't think we would give it to Geoffrey, did you?"

My cheeks flushed.

"Nellie!"

Speak of the nepo baby.

"We'll talk about it more after the holidays," Tabitha said, excusing herself just as Geoffrey sidled up next to me, twirling a hammer in his hands. *A tool with a tool. Ha!*

"This was a great idea, Nellie. Seriously, I would have never thought of this."

He nearly jumped out of his Jordans when Anita from human resources swung a sledgehammer at a desktop computer, tearing through the iridescent bow wrapped around it. Who knew the gluten-free sexagenarian had so much rage brewing inside her?

"Then again," he said. "You always come up with the best ideas."

Slack-jawed, I stared at him, taken aback by the compliment. "Wow, thank you."

"Don't look so surprised," he said around a toothy grin. "There's a reason Tabitha always pairs us up or gives me your leftovers. She knows that I can learn a lot from you."

Well, this was a startling development. A part of me was tempted to rip that ponytail clean off his head—this might be the only time I could get away with it. However, in the spirit of the holiday season and second chances, I decided to offer him a reprieve.

"Geoffrey, I've got something for you to work on. Something that we can maybe work on together after Christmas."

"What's that, Nellie Belly?"

"Boundaries." I nailed him with a pointed look. "And my name is Janelle."

He swallowed audibly. "Right. Good note." He cowered under the arch of my brow. "Janelle."

"Merry Christmas, Geoffrey."

I couldn't help but smile when he scurried off. That was nothing compared to the joy I felt when Austin stepped through the door, jumpsuit and goggles in place. I hobbled over to him, my right leg feeling more fragile than ever. It was going to take some time getting used to wearing shoes on both feet again.

"You look pretty hot in a jumpsuit," I told him.

"Oh, yeah?"

"Mm-hmm. What are you doing here?"

"Well—"

My sister stumbled through the door. "He's with me. When you told me about this place, I thought it might be the perfect opportunity for us to recreate this."

She fumbled in her pocket before drawing out an old Polaroid.

"Oh my god," I said, covering my mouth. "That wasn't one we picked out."

"I found it in an old yearbook last week."

The photo was from my seventh birthday party. I remembered it fondly, partly because of the Power Ranger piñata, but mostly because it had ended in the emergency room after I'd accidentally whacked Leighton over the head. She still had the scar to prove it.

"I thought that we should ask you first, but your sister insisted."

Austin's hesitation made me smile. It was hard to believe that this was the same guy who had fucked my face the other night. My adorable, shy alpha in disguise.

"She does that," I told him. "Let's do it."

Leighton clapped her hands together with glee. While Austin set up the shot, we picked our weapons—a crowbar for Leighton and a baseball bat for me.

"You know," I said when we were ready to go. "I'm surprised you would trust me with a bat so close to your head again."

She shrugged. "It's been twenty years. Besides, now I have a hunky boyfriend to avenge me if you take me out."

Me, too . . . I think.

I put a pin in that conversation for the next five minutes, while we beat the shit out of an animatronic Santa. By the time we were finished with him, he was slurring his words in an octave that was anything but jolly.

"Geez." Austin whistled. "What did Santa ever do to you?"

Just as I opened my mouth to sass him—because nothing riled him up quite like some back talk, and damn, did I love when he got riled up—Tabitha interrupted us.

"Janelle," she said. "I just wanted to say thank you again. I really do need to get going, but we'll talk more about Bennett Studios after the holidays."

"Sure thing, Tabitha." As if it were the most natural thing in the world, I cozied up to Austin's side, ducking my head under his arm. "You remember Austin, right?"

"Sure, your—"

"Boyfriend," I finished, even as Austin said, "Neighbor."

His body stiffened. From the corner of my eye, I saw his head whip around like something out of *The Exorcist.*

"Well, it's nice to see you again, no matter who you are." She dipped her chin in my direction. "Merry Christmas, Janelle."

"You, too."

To Austin's credit, he waited until my boss was out of earshot before asking, "Boyfriend, huh?"

"I said what I said." My cheeks flushed under the weight of his stare. "Are you up for it?"

He snaked an arm around my waist, pulling me flush against his body. I smiled when I felt the erection pressing against my front. "What do you think?"

I circled my arms around his neck. He shivered when my fingers scraped through the thin hairs there. In our few days together, most of which had been spent in bed—his bed, my bed, the bed of his truck—I had quickly learned that Austin loved to be touched.

"I think," I told him. "That I've still got a few more sick days to use before the end of the year." He groaned when I wiggled my hips, thrusting them against his cock. This was his fault; if he wanted a naughty girl, then that's what he was going to get. "Do you have any ideas for how I should spend them?"

He leaned down until his eyes were even with mine.

"I can think of a few."

Austin

"You know, this isn't exactly what I had in mind when you offered to help wrap presents."

Nellie giggled when I peeled the paper off another bow and smoothed it over her neglected nipple. "Funny," I told her, admiring my work. "Because this is exactly what I had in mind."

She climbed onto my lap and pressed her strawberry-kissed lips to mine, coaxing my mouth open with the brush of her tongue. We had been "wrapping presents" at her place for over an hour. On her couch, in her bedroom, we had even "wrapped some presents" in the kitchen while we'd waited for the Thai food to arrive, which was no doubt cold by now.

"Just so you know," she murmured against my lips. The bows dotting her nipples crinkled against my chest. "Turnabout is fair play."

"Baby, if you want to wrap a ribbon around my cock, all you have to do is ask."

She kissed me again before climbing off my lap and pulling her panties back into place. When she reached for her bra, I stopped her. "You don't need that."

"Austin," she groaned. "My parents get to town tomorrow. I really do need to wrap presents."

"Then wrap presents."

Her brows narrowed. "Like this?"

"Sure."

"In the nude?"

I shrugged. "What not?"

She chewed over my words for exactly two seconds before clapping her hands together. "Okay, then. Let's do this." Her tits bounced with every move.

Maybe I hadn't thought this one through carefully enough.

For the next hour, we *actually* wrapped presents together. Well, she wrapped while I tore off the occasional piece of tape and lent her my finger for ribbon tying. Personally, I could have thought of a lot more fun and interesting ways to utilize her ribbon, but alas, they would have to wait.

If there was one thing I had learned about Nellie, it was that she couldn't let something go until she saw it through. Just the other night, I had mentioned a new show that my nephew was obsessed with. Little had I known that by doing so, I would wake up to find a spreadsheet of gift ideas for said nephew, organized by both shipping dates and price points.

I hadn't asked her to do it. The thought had never even occurred to me, but as she'd explained it, lists and spreadsheets were her way of getting an idea out of her head and onto paper. I only wished she hadn't stayed up half the night doing so.

My little freak in the spreadsheets.

"Okay, I think that's it," she said, sitting back after the last gift was placed under the tree. "Now, about that dick ribbon."

A hearty laugh busted out of me.

"I'm just kidding," she said. "But I did have another idea."

"Anything."

"I want to take your picture."

The smile fell from my face. "Anything but that."

Her lips flattened into a thin line. "Austin."

I sighed. "Fine, but you can't put your clothes on for the rest of the night."

"Deal."

Fuck. It felt good to see her so excited. I only wished it were about anything other than taking my damn photo.

I handed over the 85 mm lens, watching as she inserted the base of it into the camera mount. She was a fast learner. We had gone over some camera basics the other night during our post-coital photo shoot under my Christmas tree. Apparently, this was turning into somewhat of a habit.

Was my naughty girl an exhibitionist?

"Where do you want me?"

She twisted her lips and searched the living room. Nellie's apartment mirrored my own, but the furniture layout couldn't have been more different. All of hers had been directed to face the fireplace and ceiling-mounted projection screen. Candles littered every surface, along with small bric-a-brac from her travels, and yet it all seemed to have a place.

Organized chaos. Just like her.

"Over there," she said, directing me to the pink slipper chair in the corner of the room.

"Okay." I planted my hands on my hips when I was finally seated. "Now what?"

She looked at me through the viewfinder. "It's missing something. One second."

My cock twitched when she bounced out of the room. That was going to make for one hell of a photo when she got back.

Me, half-mast, in a pink chair.

"Perfect." Nelly's melodic voice drifted down the hall. I clenched my jaw when she rounded the corner, this time holding my velvet Santa hat. "That'll do it," she said, plopping it on my head.

"Nellie, I—"

"Look fucking hot." She swirled a hand through my chest hair and arched her brow. "Now be a good boy and smile for me."

If only it were that easy.

Talking her through her orgasms while bending her this way and that? My pleasure. Ordering her to swallow my cock and rewarding her efforts with some light pussy taps? Simple.

But letting her lead, sitting back while all eyes were on me—even if they were just hers—was a different story.

"Hm," she said, setting the camera aside after a few shots. "I think we can do better than that. Maybe you need some inspiration."

She stood up from her spot on the rug, turned to face the kitchen, and promptly slid out of her panties. Slowly.

My blood boiled, simmering in my veins as my vision turned hazy. I sucked in a deep breath when she spun back around and removed the bows from her nipples, taking special care to play with her breasts before reaching for the camera once more. Timidness flitted across her face, but it was quickly squashed by want, unabashed hunger.

This time, I was on the menu.

Her gaze jerked down my chest, over my soft belly, to where my cock was threatening to punch a hole through my boxer briefs. I groaned when her tongue darted out to lick her lips.

"What do you want?" I palmed the outline of my cock through the fabric, hissing between clenched teeth when it throbbed against my thigh. "Tell me, Janelle."

She swallowed audibly. "I want you to touch yourself."

That's my girl.

I did as she asked, quickly yanking my briefs down my thighs before closing a fist around my hard, throbbing cock. She watched with rapt pleasure as my hand pumped up and down, humming softly when after a few strokes. I used my other hand to cup my balls.

"Janelle?"

"Wh-what?" she stammered, her cheeks now stained bright red.

"Pick up the camera, baby," I rasped. "I'm about to give you your money shot."

Chapter Ten

Nellie

Christmas Day

"Meowy Christmas."

Austin rubbed the sleep from his eyes and moved closer to me. "What did you do?" he asked, voice rich with humor.

"You wanted the traditional Wheatley family Christmas, and that begins with jolly jammies, so . . ."

I gestured toward the couch full of cats.

"That includes the whole family."

As it turned out, picking out holiday outfits for cats was a lot more fun than shopping for myself. And since I didn't believe in half-assing any task, I had gone a little overboard.

Buddy and Marley were decked out in matching red sweater vests, both of which came with remote powered lights. Technology had come a long way when it came to petwear. A small silver chain collar completed Marley's look—a nod to her namesake—while Buddy sported a striped elf hat with bells on the ends.

I had even found something for Ralphie, Austin's chonkasaurus of a feline, who had taken a special liking to me over the past few days. The green-and-red sweater with gold pom-poms was actually meant for small dogs, but neither Ralphie nor his daddy—*my daddy, too*—needed to know that.

Austin's husky laugh lit up the room, making my heart grow three sizes bigger. *Mission accomplished.* Sometime in the past week, in between large quantities of both breakfast sandwiches and orgasms, it had occurred to me that my new mission in life was to make Austin laugh.

And so far, my brilliant plan had worked out swimmingly.

He laughed while we cuddled on the couch and watched sappy holiday movies together. He laughed while watching me try on my new onesie pajamas, an early Christmas present from Leighton. He even laughed during sex, when he wasn't pounding the shit out of my pussy, that was.

That was another first for me—laughing during sex.

With Austin, sex was fun and messy, sometimes awkward. Not in a way that made me feel uncomfortable or self-conscious, except for maybe the one time my thigh cramped up while riding him reverse cowgirl. He could bend me in half and fuck my face for hours . . . so long as he did it with me on my back, preferably on a firm mattress.

#PillowPrincessForLife.

"I got you something, too."

He looked down at the wrapped box in my hand like it was a bomb instead of a gift. "You already gave me the pajamas."

Seeing as Austin and his family wouldn't be celebrating Christmas until February, I had invited him to join my family's festivities. Naturally, I had picked out a matching PJ set featuring holiday cats which showed off his belly and bulge beautifully. We would be lucky if we somehow made it through the day without me pulling him into one of the eight thousand closets at Killian and Leighton's place to suck his dick.

"Those don't count," I told him. "Everybody is required to wear pajamas. This is something just for you."

I waited eagerly as he unwrapped it, silently wishing that he loved it as much as I thought he would.

His eyes shot to mine when he rolled it over in his hand. "Nellie, I—" I waited patiently for him to find the words. "It's beautiful."

Relief flooded my body. I had spotted the vintage Santa toy in a secondhand store last week and known right away that Austin needed it in his collection. The toy's once snow-white beard had faded to a rusty brown identical to Austin's. Even more uncanny was the cat sleeping by his feet that looked just like Ralphie.

This was Santa, but it was also Austin.

Father Christmas, daddy dom, and the sweet, sensitive neighbor I had been falling for since day one, all wrapped into one.

"Get it? Because he looks like you."

Strong arms swept me up, nearly knocking over his tacky purple tree in the process. I squealed and wrapped my legs around his waist.

"Thank you so much, baby." He placed a soft, yearning kiss to my mouth. "It's perfect. You're perfect."

I couldn't contain my very unladylike snort. "We've been over this. I am *not* perfect."

"You're perfect for me."

I blinked back the tears forming in my eyes. *Damn this man and the power he has over me.* He squeezed a handful of my ass when I didn't respond right away.

"This is the part where you say, 'You're perfect for me, too, Austin.'"

"And miss out on an opportunity for you to punish me?"

The hardening cock against my center was all the answer I needed.

"How long before we need to be at your sister's house?"

"Forty minutes." Rather than ravage me then and there, as I expected him to, he closed his eyes. "What are you doing?"

An adorable crease formed between his brows. "I'm calculating all the ways I could make you come in less than forty minutes."

Mmm, sexy math.

I hummed when his palms kneaded my ass, rubbing me against his burgeoning erection. "And what did you decide on?"

His eyes sprung open.

"I decided we're going to be late."

Austin

The Wheatleys kicked ass.

Literally. They were kicking my ass at every fucking game.

Even Nellie and Leighton's parents, Hank and Wanda. The pair had at least two-and-a-half decades on the rest of us, and yet here they were, running circles around both Killian—a retired, professional soccer player—and me.

Time to haul my ass back to the gym.

Christmas looked a lot different here than it did in the Amato household, starting with the matching pajamas over brunch and ending with the Minute-to-Win-It-style tournament, aptly named the Wheatley Winter Games. For two hours, we had stacked cups, flung candy canes, and used straws to blow jingle bells from one end of the coffee table to the other.

One by one, I had lost them all. Hell, I had nearly taken an elbow to the groin during *Holiday Nutstacker*.

Talk about a great "meet the parents" story.

Despite my humiliation and utter lack of athleticism, I was having the time of my life.

Wanda had taken to me immediately, insisting that I be her partner for the first two games. At first, I'd thought it might have been because of how much she loved her gift. Nellie and Leighton had turned the photos we had taken together into a calendar for their parents, each month featuring side-by-side then and now pictures. Wanda had opened the present after breakfast and promptly burst into tears. Hank, on the other hand, had simply nodded his head and said something akin to, "That's nice."

Nellie assured me that that was as good as a standing ovation.

During a brief boozy coffee break, she had also confided in me the real reason her mother wanted to be my partner.

"She thinks you look like David Harbour, her celebrity hall pass."

"The guy from *Stranger Things*?"

She nodded. "He also did a movie where he dressed like Santa."

I laughed when she wagged her brows suggestively. Apparently, she wasn't the only Wheatley woman who had a thing for the big man in red.

We had just moved on to playing the last game, *Snowballing*, when my phone vibrated across the table. Nellie smiled when I flashed her the name on screen. "Tell her hi from me."

I excused myself to the patio and answered Sloane's call.

"Merry Christmas, buddy."

"Merry Christmas, boss."

A slurp from the other end of the phone gave me pause. "What are you doing?"

"Eating ramen and watching football. Duh."

"Since when are you a football fan?"

"Um, since forever. Have you seen how tight their pants are?"

I rolled my eyes and peeked through the sliding glass door. "I can't talk long, but I'm glad you called. Nellie says hello. She just landed that account I told you about, so she wants to throw a little celebratory dinner thing next week. You're invited."

"Count me in."

Bennett Studios had officially inked their deal with Wilson, Treger, and Faison two days ago, just in time for Christmas. In addition, all three partners had unanimously decided that Nellie would lead the account. Obviously, she was thrilled, and I was thrilled for her. She was the hardest working person I knew, so she deserved to be recognized for the fruits of her labor.

"Damn, Brooks Bennett," she said wistfully. "He was my first celebrity crush. I used to kiss his poster every night before bed."

"You want me to hook you up?"

"I wish." She laughed through the phone. "On second thought, ask me again in six months."

"What about Laric?"

From what she had told me before, Laric already had Christmas plans with family. Sloane was going to join them in Joshua Tree for New Year's Eve.

"He's fine."

I waited for her to elaborate. The pit forming in my stomach snowballed out of control when I heard her sniffle instead.

"Sloane—"

"I'm okay, big man. We can talk later. You have your *girlfriend's* parents to impress." I couldn't help but smile when she used the word *girlfriend*. I had a girlfriend. Fuck, I sounded like a gangly preteen. "I just wanted to wish you a Merry Christmas and tell you I'm happy for you."

"Thanks, Slo."

We said our goodbyes, and I made a mental note to check in with her again tomorrow. Something was off with Sloane, and I needed to know what.

But there was something that had to happen first.

I snuck back inside the house and grabbed my camera, returning to the living room just as Killian tossed the final snowball—aka, a plastic Easter egg painted white—to Leighton. She jumped up and down when the timer went off, excited yet unaware of what was still to come.

When Killian's gaze found mine from across the room, I nodded.

"Check the egg, princess," Killian said, his voice shaking. I had never seen the man so nervous before.

"You know perfectly well it's a *snowball*, killjoy."

"Check it," he repeated.

Her eyes widened when she snapped the egg open, and then filled with tears when Killian removed the diamond ring from inside and got down on one knee.

"Leighton, not a day goes by when I don't find something new to add to the list of reasons why I love you." Tears of joy streamed down her cheeks. "Please, do me the honor of giving me more time to love you, hold you, and, hopefully, spend the rest of my life trying to make you as happy as you make me. Will you marry me?"

"Yes!" she screamed, wrapping her arms around his neck and tackling him to the floor. Nellie and her parents cheered, peppering the couple with tearful hugs and kisses when they finally came up for air.

And all the while, I watched it through my viewfinder.

Later, after Hank and Wanda had retired to the guest room to take a postgame nap and Killian and Leighton had disappeared for a private celebration, I pulled Nellie aside for a private moment of our own.

"You know," she said once we were safely tucked away inside the laundry room. "As much as I love where your head's at, there are much better rooms in the house. *Bigger* rooms with padded carpet."

I couldn't contain my shit-eating grin . . . or the erection straining against my boxer briefs. We could christen every fucking room in the house if she wanted to, but it was going to have to wait.

Her eyes sparkled with interest when I handed her the leather-bound album. "This is for you."

"Austin, you didn't have to—"

"Get my girlfriend a present for Christmas?" She rolled her eyes. "I meant to give it to you this morning when it was just the two of us, but then we got a little distracted."

She opened the album and froze. "How did you—"

"I had a little help."

I didn't need to look at the photos again. They were already permanently etched in my brain—all sixteen of them. Instead, I studied Nellie, absorbing every emotional reaction as she experienced them for the first time.

There was the one we had taken on my living room floor the night we'd first had sex. I had cropped her pert nipples out of the frame, but it was hard to miss the beads of sweat dotting our skin. She turned the page, smiling when she reached our photo in the snow globe. Sloane deserved a fucking bonus for that one. Much to my surprise, she had adjusted the focus, effectively blurring the rest of the background and drawing your eyes straight to Nellie and me, who only had eyes for each other.

There were candid photos, too—from our photo shoots, the rage room, even one or two from the pet store. I watched as she flipped through page after page, smiling ear to ear as she relived a series of snapshots in time that, collectively, told our story.

When she reached the last page, her eyes widened, twinkling with lust. "Holy shit," she whispered. "That is so fucking hot."

I didn't need to see it to know that she was talking about the one of me jerking off in her chair. Going through the film had been an enlightening experience. Nellie had been . . . thorough, to say the least. This particular photo, though, had called to me. It was the perfect blend of dominance and submission, a man hungering for control but beholden to the woman he loved.

Damn, I was getting hard just thinking about it.

"Thank you, so much," she said, clutching the book to her chest. "You don't know what this means to me."

I kissed a fallen tear from her cheek. "You don't know what you mean to me."

There was nothing left to say after that. Not with words anyway. We let our tongues do the talking. I snaked a hand underneath her skirt, teasing the crease of her panties. She was already wet for me. She whimpered when I pulled my hand away, then jolted against my lips when I brought it back down, lightly slapping her clit.

"Now," I said between kisses. "What were you saying about padded carpet?"

Epilogue

Valentine's Day

Nellie

I might never eat fish again.

Austin hadn't been joking when he'd told me about the Amato family's Feast of Twelve Fishes. In fact, it was thirteen dishes, by my count. There were fish I had never even heard of before.

"Will somebody pass the perch, please?"

That was one of them. What the hell was a perch, and why did it taste so good coated in brown butter?

"So, Janelle." I turned my attention toward Char, Austin's oldest sister. Something told me that she could give Tabitha a run for her money when it came to intimidation tactics. "Do you still have family in Ohio?"

"Definitely. In fact, my sister and I are really the only ones who moved away."

"And you both settled in L.A.?"

She eyed my plate suspiciously. I had done my best to move around what was left so it looked like I'd eaten more, but apparently not well enough. "She moved to L.A. about a decade before I did, but yes. Now we live within a few miles of each other."

"Do you hear that?" This time, the question was directed toward her sisters, Madi and Sav. "Janelle doesn't *abandon* her sister, like some people I know."

"My restaurant is in Boston," Madi whined. "What am I supposed to do?"

"What's your excuse, Miss Florida?"

Sav shrugged. "The beaches are better."

Thankful that Char had directed her ire elsewhere and that her inquisition was over—at least for now—I pivoted in my seat to face the kitchen. Austin had disappeared at least ten minutes ago, supposedly to fetch more gravy, but now I wasn't so sure

"He's just changing," Austin's mom whispered from the seat beside me.

"Did he spill or something?"

She shook her head and smiled. "He's putting on his *other* suit."

His Santa suit.

I nodded with understanding.

"You know," I said softly, "I've seen him in action in his *other* suit, and he's absolutely incredible. He has a real gift." And because I knew Austin would never talk himself up, especially not to his family, I went on singing his praises. "His photographs, too. Did you know that one of them is going to be on the cover of a magazine next month? He never ceases to amaze me."

She stared back at me, bewildered. There was something else there, too. Pride, maybe. And why not? She should be proud of her son and the person he had become, the man she had raised him to be.

"Thank you."

I blinked, taken aback. "For what?"

"For being the partner that my son deserves."

Fuck. I cursed myself when I felt my eyes water. This was not the time or the place. I refused to cry over shrimp scampi and cod lasagna.

"Please, do me a favor." Austin's mom covered my hand with hers. "Be sure to tell him so every day."

I do. "I will."

She patted my hand. "Now, pass me the mussels, honey."

Talk about one hell of a weird Valentine's Day, that was for sure. Not quite the nonstop fuckfest I had envisioned for my first Valentine's Day with a boyfriend, but still, the night was young.

Austin and I had the entire basement all to ourselves, and there was a brand-new lace teddy burning a hole in my carry-on suitcase.

"Ho, ho, ho."

Yes. Yes, I am.

Austin descended the stairs dressed in full Santa garb, white gloves and all. His nieces and nephews rushed from the dinner table to greet him, followed quickly by the rest of the family.

I hadn't been exaggerating when I'd told his mom he had a gift. I stood back, poised against the wall covered in childhood photos, watching him engage with the children. How he was able to give each of them his undivided attention, one at a time, was beyond me.

It was when he was halfway through handing out gifts that the primal urge came over me.

Maybe it was the velvet.

Maybe it was the leather boots.

Maybe it was the fact that he was good with kids and that made me want to do stupid things, like beg him to put a baby inside me.

Whatever the case, I knew that I had to have him now.

White gloves and all.

Austin

"Dear Santa, you might be surprised to know that I've been a bad girl this year. And as we both know, naughty girls must be punished."

I turned the paper into my chest when my two-year-old nephew came streaking through the kitchen in the buff.

"Madison," I shouted down the hall. "Your kid is naked."

"Oh, for fuck's sake," she grumbled, chasing after him.

I waited until the sound of their footsteps disappeared before opening up Nellie's note again. She had slipped it into the pocket of my Santa coat nearly an hour ago before disappearing down the basement steps. Thankfully, I had waited to read it until after the kids—minus my naked nephew—had gone to bed. It would have been mighty difficult to hide an erection in this suit.

"Somebody once told me that only good girls get what they want for Christmas, but I'm hoping you'll make an exception, just this once."

I groaned, palming my greedy cock through the velvet pants. Role-playing aside, Nellie knew that I would give her anything she wanted, plus a healthy dose of what she needed. All she had to do was ask.

"All I want for Christmas is you, Santa. Fuck me, use me, fill me up with your cum. Tonight, I'm your toy. I'll be waiting downstairs, in a special outfit I picked specifically for you."

I took off for the basement like an animal unleashed. It took all of ten seconds to reach the bottom step, and when I did, I nearly came in my pants. That would have made for one hell of an awkward trip to the dry cleaners.

There she was—my naughty girl—standing in the middle of my sister's rumpus room, wearing nothing but a scrape of red lace . . . and faux white fur trim. She might as well have been naked. *She will be soon.* Even under the glow of the twinkle lights strung around the room's perimeter, I could see the patch of hair between her thighs and the pretty pink nipples threatening to break through her teddy.

"Did you read my letter, Santa?" she asked, batting her long eyelashes at me.

"I did."

"And?"

Nellie bit her lip coyly, waiting to see what came next.

"And I think it's time that Santa taught you what happens to girls on the naughty list. Come here."

She slunk toward me, her hips swaying hypnotically. My breath caught when she ran her fingers down my chest, toying with the edges of my coat.

"Did I say you could touch me?" I growled, grabbing her wrist. "On your knees."

Nellie's eyes widened, a mixture of fear and excitement flashing across her face. She hesitated for just a moment before slowly sinking to her knees, her gaze never leaving mine.

"My naughty girl," I said, my voice low and husky.

With my free hand, I slowly undid the buttons of my red coat, revealing the bare skin beneath. I was suddenly grateful I had decided to forgo the undershirt tonight. I guessed I had Char to thank for that one; she kept her thermostat higher than Death Valley six months of the year.

Nellie's gaze dropped, drinking in the sight hungrily.

"Eyes up here," I commanded, giving her silky hair a sharp tug. She gasped, her attention snapping back to my face. "Now, I think it's time you showed Santa just how sorry you are for being so naughty."

I released her hair and stepped to the corner of the room, sitting down in the plush armchair that was typically covered in kids' toys and extra blankets. Spreading my legs wide, I beckoned her forward with one finger.

"Come here and unwrap your present."

Nellie crawled toward me, her movements slow and deliberate. When she reached me, her trembling hands moved to my belt buckle, her eyes locked on mine the whole time. Slowly, seductively, she un-buckled it, her soft fingers brushing against the erection tenting my pants. A low growl escaped my lips as anticipation coursed through me.

"That's it," I rasped. "Take it out, baby girl."

With a shaky exhale, Nellie pulled down my pants and boxer briefs, revealing my hard length. Her eyes widened, but she didn't flinch. Instead, she leaned forward and ran her tongue along the swollen head of my cock, sending shivers down my spine.

"Beg for it."

"*Please.*"

"Please, what?"

"Please, Daddy," she purred. "Please let me have your cock."

I couldn't hold back any longer, not when she was asking nicely.

With a growl, I grabbed a fistful of her hair and guided her mouth.. Looking up at me again with big, beautiful eyes, she placed her hands on my thighs before leaning in and licking a stripe up the underside of my throbbing cock.

"*Fuck,*" I hissed.

She went back for seconds, tasting the bead of precum leaking from my slit. My hips gave an involuntary thrust when she gave a soft, little hum, like she enjoyed the flavor.

"You can take more of me, baby."

Nellie moaned around me as I pushed deeper, her lips stretching to accommodate my girth.

"That's it, baby girl, take it all."

She bobbed her head eagerly, her tongue swirling around my shaft as she sucked. The sight of her on her knees, still in that lacy Santa number, was almost too much to bear. I gripped the armrests of the chair, fighting the urge to thrust up into her warm, wet mouth.

As Nellie worked her magic, I lost myself in the sensations. Her tongue swirling around my length, the gentle scrape of her teeth, the way her throat constricted around me when she took me deep—it was exquisite torture. I could feel the pressure building, threatening to overwhelm me.

I groaned again, my self-control rapidly unraveling. She kept going, sucking and licking. When she cupped my balls, I knew I had reached my limit.

The gloves came off.

"Stop," I growled, gently drawing her head back.

Nellie whimpered, her lips swollen and glistening. "What's wrong, Daddy?"

"Nothing, baby. Your mouth is fucking incredible, but I'm not finished with you yet."

With a swift motion, I pulled her up and tossed her over my shoulder, relishing her squeal of surprise and delight.

A sharp crack to her ass made her yelp.

"This is your punishment, remember?"

In one fluid motion, I dumped her onto the bed, coming down on top of her. She gasped as I roughly spread her legs, exposing her dripping center. The scrap of lace that passed for panties was soaked through.

"Look how wet you are for me," I murmured, running a finger along her slit.

I teased her entrance, feeling her hips buck against my hand. Nellie whimpered, her eyes pleading.

"*Please, Daddy*. I need you inside me."

"Patience, baby girl," I growled, slowly circling her clit. "You've been naughty, remember? Naughty girls don't get what they want right away."

She buried her face in the pillow when I dipped two fingers inside her, relishing how tight and wet she felt. We were going to wake the whole house up at this rate, and yet, I couldn't be bothered to care.

Nellie moaned, arching her back as I pumped my fingers in and out at an agonizingly slow pace, swirling them up and back against her G-spot.

"More, please," she begged, her hands fisting the sheets.

I smirked, enjoying her desperate pleas. "More what, baby girl? Use your words."

"More . . . everything." Her hips rocked against my hand. "Faster, harder."

I obliged, increasing the pace of my fingers and adding a third. The wet sounds of her arousal filled the room.

"That's it," I growled, feeling her inner walls start to clench. "Come for me."

With a strangled moan, Nellie came undone. Her body shook as waves of pleasure washed over her. I worked her through it, only slowing my movements when she whimpered from oversensitivity.

As she lay there panting, I positioned myself between her legs.

I lined up my throbbing cock with her entrance, still slick and sensitive from her orgasm. Slowly, I pushed inside, savoring every inch as her tight heat enveloped me.

Nellie gasped, digging her nails under my coat and into my back as I filled her completely.

"God, I'll never get tired of having you like this, feeling you wrapped around me." Her legs tightened around my waist, pulling me closer still. "I love you so fucking much."

She stilled. We both did.

It was safe to say that this probably wasn't how either of us had pictured saying those words for the first time. It wasn't every day that you told the love of your life how you felt about her while balls deep and dressed like Santa. Which was why we both burst out laughing.

"I love you, too."

Her pussy contracted around my cock with each spurt of laughter, making me groan. The urge to taste her was too much to resist. My heart thudded in my chest, my pulse pounding as I found her lips.

"Now fuck me like you love me, Santa."

I didn't need to be told twice. I started with slow, deep thrusts, relishing the way her walls clenched around me. Nellie moaned softly with each roll of my hips, her nails digging into my shoulders.

"Harder," she pleaded.

Growling, I picked up the pace, slamming into her with abandon. The room filled with the sound of skin slapping against skin, punctuated by our shared moans of pleasure. Nellie's head fell back, exposing the long line of her throat. I couldn't resist leaning down to nip and suck at the sensitive skin there, leaving my mark.

"Oh, fuck yes."

Her legs tightened around me, heels digging into my lower back as she urged me deeper. I gripped her hips, angling them upward to hit that spot inside her that I knew would make her see stars.

When her inner walls fluttered around my cock, I skimmed a hand up her throat and squeezed.

"Come for me again, baby," I growled in her ear. "I want to feel you come on my cock."

Her back arched as she cried out, her orgasm crashing over her. The pulsing of her pussy around me was too much to bear. With a guttural moan, I buried myself to the hilt inside her and let go, my release pulsing deep within her trembling body. We clung to each other, panting and shuddering through the aftershocks.

Slowly, I released my grip on her throat and pressed a tender kiss to her flushed cheek. Nellie's eyes fluttered open, pupils still blown wide with pleasure. A satisfied smile curved her lips as she ran her fingers through my sweat-dampened hair.

"That was . . . ," she breathed.

"Incredible," I finished, freeing myself from the scratchy polyester beard before capturing her mouth in a languid kiss.

We lay there in comfortable silence for a while, basking in the afterglow. Eventually, Nellie propped herself up on an elbow to look at me, a mischievous glint in her eye.

"Ready for round two?" she asked. "Assuming Mrs. Claus isn't waiting up for you."

"She'll be waiting a long time," I told her, pulling her lips back to mine.

"Merry Christmas, Austin," she whispered.

"Happy Valentine's Day, Janelle."

Thanks for Reading!

Thank you so much for reading *Santa Monica Baby!*

Nellie and Austin's book took a while to figure out, mostly because I knew who she was (we met her in *Venice Actually)* but it took a while to figure out who would win her heart. All I knew was that she needed a big boy. Then came Santa, *then* came Austin, and that was all she wrote.

This isn't goodbye for these characters. In fact . . .

Stay tuned for Sloane's story in 2025, in my brand new spin-off series, THE DESERT DADDIES.

If you liked this novella, please let me know and share with others by leaving a review on **Amazon** or **Goodreads :)**

Acknowledgements

Truth be told, this one was hard to write. But, I suppose that's what I get for trying to write a sweet and spicy novella during an election year! Thankfully, I'm luckier than most in that I have a thriving community beside me 24/7.

Mamasita, you've always been my number one reader, and for that, I will always be grateful. And even though I know you will probably *never* read my books, Papa Bear—which is probably for the best for all of us—you still deserve big praise for answering all of my random baseball questions.

To my amazing editor, Norma. Thank you for your notes and more importantly, your flexibility. You always put up with me no matter how many times I change the release date.

As always, shoutout to the chat groups that keep me sane and entertained—you all know who you are and how much you mean to me. Thank you for the hours of input, memes, incessant questions (mine, not yours) and TikTok videos.

To the baristas at Cathedral Coffee and Daydreamer in Portland, Oregon, thank you for the coffee and writing space.

Finally, to the romance readers, and every person who has supported Boobies & Noobies over the years, thank you for welcoming me into your community. Every day, I am more and more thankful I picked up that copy of *I'm in No Mood for Love* by Rachel Gibson back in 2009. Who knows where I'd be or what I'd be doing today if I hadn't. Above all else, Boobies & Noobies has always been a podcast about exploring readers and writers' unique romance reading journeys. Thank you all for being a part of *my* romance reading (and writing) journey.

Here's to another fifteen years of HEAs.

About the Author

By day, Kelly Reynolds works primarily as a freelance writer, professor, and author's assistant. By night, she hosts the romance novel review podcast, Boobies & Noobies. She currently lives in Portland, Oregon. When she isn't writing, you can often find Kelly eating her way through hole-in-the-wall restaurants, sampling cider at the nearest brewery, or bingeing the latest season of "Top Chef".

Keep up with Kelly on social media @authorkellyrey (Instagram, Twitter, and Threads), @realkellyrey (Tiktok), and on her website.

Keep up with Boobies & Noobies on social media @boobiespodcast, and listen wherever you stream your podcasts.